DIRTY LITTLE Secrets

CASSIE CROSS

This is a work of fiction. Names, characters, places, and incidents are a product of the author's imagination. Locales and public names are sometimes used for atmospheric purposes. Any resemblance to actual people, living or dead, or to businesses, companies, events, institutions, or locales is completely coincidental.

Cover design by Mayhem Cover Creations

Interior Design and Formatting by:

www.emtippettsbookdesigns.com

For the latest news on upcoming releases, please visit

CassieCross.com

CHAPTER *One*

"You look so hot in that dress. I just want to put my mouth all over you."

The voice comes from behind me, and is too close to my ear for its owner to be talking to anyone but me. I steady myself for the reveal, because I know that when I turn around to let this guy off easy, I'm going to be looking into the face of a disgusting, smarmy barfly who thinks that's the kind of compliment that's going to get me to go home with him.

No "Hello, nice to meet you." No "Let me buy you a drink." He just goes straight for the kill, which I suppose is a blessing. At least I know what he wants from me right away.

I shift uncomfortably in my seat in the middle of the not-so-crowded hotel bar, and turn to face the man who just spoke to me. He reeks of booze, even though happy hour is still in its infancy. He's disheveled and greasy, and he's looking at me like I'm some kind of dessert. My gaze drifts over his shoulder, looking around to see if I notice anyone suspicious. He could be some kind of a decoy to distract me, for all I know.

I don't get any bad vibes from anyone in the room, apart from this guy, and there's no way I'm giving him the time of day. That's bad news for him, because I'm probably the most desperate woman he'll find in this bar tonight. Hell, I might just be the most desperate woman in the city. I'm on the run from a dangerous man who probably wants me dead. I'm low on cash, and scared I'll run out before I figure a way out of the mess I've managed to get myself into, and I don't know where I'll be staying after tomorrow night.

Despite all that, even *I'm* not desperate enough to go home with this guy, even if it will buy me a few hours of oblivion and a little bit of safety.

With the toe of my shoe, I shift my bag beneath my barstool, making sure it's still there. I've got one of its straps wrapped around my ankle, so I'll know if anyone tries to take it. I'm hyper-vigilant about theft of my belongings anyway, but everything I managed to pack before I hastily left my apartment in Chicago is in this bag.

It's all I've got for now, so I've got to keep a close eye on it. If I lose it, I might as well turn myself over to the man who is looking for me. His name is Andre Privya, and it's not a question of *if* he'll find me, it's *when*. I'm just hoping that I'll be able to come up with a way to get myself out of his crosshairs before that inevitable moment comes.

"Did you hear what I said?" Douchebag asks.

I left Chicago three days ago under the cloak of night, and I've been here in Manhattan ever since. In that time, I think my fight-or-flight response has served me well. This guy doesn't exactly scream "hitman" to me, but I know I should steer clear of him if only because he seems like a gross, terrible person.

"I did," I reply, stirring my drink. I've got to keep a close eye on that, and make sure he doesn't slip me something. He seems like the type who would. "I'm flattered, but I'm not interested."

Douchebag looks annoyed, like I expected he would, but he isn't willing to back down just yet. "Let me buy you a drink and see if I can change your mind."

I look him right in the eyes and say, "No."

He's got this smirk on his stupid, smarmy face, and I know he thinks that I'm playing hard to get. He thinks this is game, and he's sure he's going to win. "Bartender," he says, raising his hand.

I shake my head. "No. I don't want a drink."

"C'mon, just-"

"She said *no*." A hand claps down hard on Douchebag's shoulder, right before he is whirled around to face what has to be one of the handsomest men I've ever seen in my life. Handsome and full of righteous anger, which I'm finding incredibly attractive, I'm not ashamed to admit. "Do you understand what 'no' means?"

Douchebag nods shakily. "Y-yes."

"Then why are you still standing here?"

Just like that, Douchebag hightails it out of the bar, and into the hotel's lobby.

"Is everything okay?" This gorgeous man is looking at me with such concern in his soulful green eyes, and I can't seem to find my voice.

All I can do is nod slowly, taking in the view before me. He is really, incredibly tall. And from the looks of it, he's broad and muscular, but unfortunately his well-tailored suit is hiding a lot of the aforementioned muscles, just giving me the slightest hint of what is waiting below in the way it hugs his body. He has a head full of light brown hair with a few highlights mixed in, like he has just spent some time out in the sun. His eyes are friendly, and way too easy to get lost in.

I shouldn't be getting lost in anyone's eyes right now; it could be dangerous. Strangely, though, I don't feel like I'm in danger with him.

"Yes," I finally manage to say. "I'm fine. Thank you for that."

He smiles, and that smile is too easy to get lost in, as well. Why did this stupidly beautiful man have to show up here, now, when I absolutely cannot afford to let myself get swept off of my feet? Why couldn't I have met someone like him in Chicago? If I hadn't left town, if I hadn't done such an idiotic, dangerous thing…

"You have nothing to thank me for," he replies. "I hate that we live in a world where my 'no' carries more weight than yours does."

Oh, he's good. It's a little difficult to get a read on him, but I don't think he's feeding me a line here. I want to believe him, that much is true.

"I'm going to grab a drink. Can I get you anything?"

"No," I reply, tapping my glass. "I'm good, thank you."

"Would you like some company, or-"

"Yes," I reply without even a moment's hesitation. "I'd love some company." He's handsome and friendly, and I suppose it's better to be safe than sorry, just in case the guy who was just hitting on me decides to come back. I'd also like to be in this man's presence for a little while longer, strange as that seems. I'm just not ready for him to leave yet.

"What's your name?" he asks.

"Mia." Immediately I wonder if I should've given him a fake name. That probably would've been the smart thing to do, but it's too late now.

"It's a pleasure to meet you, Mia," he says, offering me his hand. I reach out and take it, feeling a little thrill shoot through me when we touch. "I'm Caleb."

"It's nice to meet you."

"I'll be right back," he tells me, his hand lingering in mine until he absolutely has to pull away.

My stomach swoops as he walks away, and I'm in trouble,

I know it. It's not the kind of trouble I've been running away from for the past three days, though; it's the kind of trouble that makes me want to run toward it, full speed, even though I know it's probably a terrible idea.

While Caleb walks over to the other side of the bar, he watches me out of the corner of his eye. I'm not sure if he's doing it because he thinks I'm going to get up and walk away, or because he wants to make sure the guy who was hitting on me doesn't return. Either way, I feel comforted in a way that I haven't since I figured out that Privya and his goons were onto me, and I needed to get out of Chicago as soon as possible.

Caleb glances my way from the bar, and he smiles at me. It's not the sweet, helpful smile that he gave me earlier, when he was dispatching the douchebag. No, this smile has heat behind it; it makes the hairs on my arms stand on end with anticipation. This smile makes me *want* him. Badly.

Despite my body's apparent desire to get completely swept up by this man's charms and looks, my mind keeps replaying this niggling thought that this could be some kind of trap. Maybe I'm not as on top of Privya and his whereabouts as I think I am. My computer skills are stellar—which is how I got myself into this mess in the first place—but there's the slightest chance that I'm wrong about where he is. I've been planting false trails around Chicago to fool him into thinking that I haven't left town. What if he's doing the same?

I'm reasonably sure that Privya wouldn't go so far as to

have one of his men hit on me in a bar. If he has enough intel on me to know I'm staying in this hotel, then he'd just show up at my door and kidnap me or something. Men like him don't have much finesse, they just see their objective and take aim. Besides, any professional criminal would never leave me alone, giving me the chance to escape, while he went to the bar to get himself some scotch.

No, this is just a handsome man with a good streak in him. I shouldn't look into it any more than that.

I catch Caleb's eye while he's in the middle of a conversation with the bartender that I can tell he desperately wants to get out of. I attempt a seductive slide off of my barstool, if such a thing is even possible, then reach down and grab my bag. Caleb's face brightens when he sees me heading his way, and I can *feel* him watching me. It's not the look of a man who is after me for things that I've done, it's the look of a man who wants to do things *to* me. Filthy, wonderful things. The look is…it's too much. It sends a jolt of anticipatory panic through my veins, and like a coward, I take a detour and head left.

Right into the ladies' room.

There isn't anyone in here, thankfully, and I take a second to stare at my reflection in the mirror. With chocolate brown hair, hazel eyes, and my head held high, no one would take me for a coward. No one would take me for a criminal, either, though I'm definitely one of those now. Even though I stole from a terrible person for noble reasons, I'm still a thief, aren't

I?

An impulsive, cowardly thief.

I have a man who is looking at me like he wants to devour me, and I walk into the bathroom? How I've ever managed to get laid is beyond me.

I want to go back to the bar and talk to Caleb. I want to see where this thing between us goes. I need this. I need the stress relief. I want it, too. I want to lose myself in the arms of a handsome stranger, even if it is just for one night.

Running my fingers through my hair, I take a deep, cleansing breath. What do I have to lose if I spend one night with him?

As long as he's not one some kind of a decoy, absolutely nothing.

No, he's not a decoy. He's not. I know it in my bones.

I readjust my bag on my shoulder before I make my way back into the bar. I don't see Caleb at first, but then I feel his fingertips slide along the crook inside my elbow. The touch is light, but full of intent. He wants me to turn around, but he doesn't want to force it.

I stop—of course I stop—and he moves in, like he's going to tell me a secret.

Whatever it is he has to say, I have never wanted to hear something so badly in my entire life.

"Don't walk away from me, Mia," he whispers. His voice is low and firm, but there's an undercurrent of pleading in it.

I couldn't walk away if I tried.

CHAPTER *Two*

"You have really nice hands," I say, before I can stop myself. "It was nice when you touched me." I shake my head as I try to get my stupid, nervous mouth under control. "What I mean is that it felt good, like…never mind."

"Mia," Caleb laughs, leaning in close. Just the way he says my name sends a thrill to all the right places, and his hot breath on my skin combined with the way his lips brush the shell of my ear make me shiver. "You have no idea how good my hands can feel."

I take a deep breath, not daring to look at him. I'm a little weak, and I'm worried that I'm going to embarrass myself, because I know that Caleb felt me tremble just now.

"Are you here with someone?" he asks.

Does he want to know if I came to the bar with someone,

or if I'm here at the hotel with someone? I suppose it doesn't matter either way, because the answer is, "No."

His lips lift up into a grin at my answer, and I lean in a little closer, wanting to be near the warmth of his body. He smells good, and he's so gorgeous; it's like every single cell in my body is a magnet, pulling me to him. I want to wrap my arms around him, I want to bury my face in his neck and breathe deep. I can't even bring myself to worry about the fact that I'm practically intoxicated by this man that I've only just met. It's insane, and yet here I am.

"Are you here with anyone?"

"No."

I grin, kind of like he did just now.

"Your smile is gorgeous," he says.

My apparently gorgeous smile grows bigger. "My dad paid a lot of money or it," I say. I immediately want to smack my hand over my mouth, because I'm drunk on pheromones, and I'm going to wind up making a huge fool of myself because of it. "I mean, he didn't pay for veneers or anything; these are my actual teeth. I meant braces. He paid for braces." I shake my head once I finally stop talking, feeling the blush rising in my cheeks. I want to duck behind the bar and hide, but I'll settle for bringing my hands up to my face to act as a shield because I'm so embarrassed.

There's a shift in the air. I can tell that Caleb is moving closer, and then his arm brushes mine. "Don't do that," he says, his voice rough in my ear. He crooks his fingers around my wrists and gives them a gentle tug. "Don't cover your face."

I can't deny his request, and when my hands drop to my sides, I give him a smile. It's almost too much to believe that this beautiful man is as into me as I'm into him, even though he's saying all the right things, and looking at me with unbridled heat in his eyes.

When he reaches up and slides his thumb across my cheekbone, it's like the smallest touch sets my skin on fire.

"Beautiful," Caleb whispers, like it's a secret between the two of us.

"You're good at this." My voice sounds more affected than I expected it to, and the flash of lust in Caleb's eyes lets me know that he noticed it.

"Good at what?"

I playfully roll my eyes. I'm practically putty in his hands, and he's acting like he doesn't know what I'm talking about. "You know, the whole seduction thing."

He flashes that killer smile, and I'm expecting that the next words out of his mouth are going to be utterly, ridiculously cocky.

"I like you," is all he says. No smooth line, just straight and to the point.

"You haven't known me long enough to know if you like me." That is totally not true, but if he knew the reason why I'm here in this hotel, in this city, he probably wouldn't like me very much. Especially since Caleb exudes the kind of confidence that only rich men seem to have. I'm guessing he wouldn't be too impressed if I told him that in an impulsive moment of anger, I fancied myself a modern-day Robin Hood.

"I have known you long enough, and I do like you."

I'm choosing to believe him, because why not? If this thing goes anywhere, it's one night at most. It would be a nice respite, and a reprieve from the running. He is way, *way* out of my league, so I would be foolish not to take this chance while I have it. I reach out and take Caleb's hand, and if he's shocked by that, he doesn't let on. I turn it in my grip, and uncurl his fingers, bringing the back of his hand to rest against my thigh. My fingertip traces the lines that stretch across his palm. His hands are calloused, something I wasn't expecting from a man wearing such a nice suit. I figured typing was the most work he did with his hands, but now I want to feel the roughness of them gliding across the planes of my body.

"What are you doing?" Caleb asks, his voice stilted.

Grinning, I reply, "I'm tracing your like line."

Caleb looks so adorably confused. "My what?"

"When I was a kid, my grandmother lived across the street from a palm reader," I explain, as my finger continues its circuit. "I was obsessed with her; I thought she was the coolest person I'd ever seen. She wore these long, flowing dresses, and kept her hair all wrapped up in these bright silk scarves. Anyway, my grandmother, of course, thought everything that came out of this woman's mouth was complete bullshit."

When I look up, Caleb is watching me intently with his never-ending green eyes. I have to take a deep breath to steady myself before I continue.

"One summer, my grandmother told me to stop bothering the woman, and taught me to read my own palm." I glide my finger along the line that stretches from above Caleb's thumb, down to the heel of his hand. "She used to call this the 'like line.' Allegedly it's supposed to be an indicator of how long you're going to live, but she told me it was a good way to tell if someone is an asshole or not."

Caleb lets out an infectious, genuine laugh. "What's mine showing you?"

I cradle his hand in mine, and make a show of examining his palm. Part of the reason is because I want to keep touching him for as long as I possibly can, and I think he might be on to me. I feel safe here, with him. It's the safest I've felt since I came to this damned city.

"I think you're good," I reply, not letting go.

"These hands can show you other things," he says after a moment, his voice very soft and inviting.

I want those hands to show me everything, to touch me everywhere. The problem is that I don't know how to tell him what I want. Will a simple, 'yes, please' work?

Ultimately, I decide to be honest. "I don't know how to do this."

"Do what?"

"Have casual sex."

Caleb flips his hand over, covers my knee with it, then trails his fingers up, up, up my thigh until his fingertips dance along the slit of my dress. He takes the fabric and gently slides it between his fingers. It's such a simple gesture, but I'm transfixed by it until he slides off the barstool, then reaches into his pocket, and pulls out his wallet.

He leaves a giant tip for the bartender, then leans in. Close.

I think my heart stops beating.

"Mia," he whispers. Nothing on this earth could tear my attention away from him. Goosebumps erupt all over my skin, like my body knows that no one has ever said words that are as important as the ones Caleb is about to say to me. "Sex with you could never be casual."

CHAPTER *Three*

"You're on the twenty-fifth floor, huh?" Caleb asks. He's looking down at me, and licking his lips.

"Mmm-hmm." I slide my fingertip down the edge of the lapel of his jacket, fantasizing about what his chest looks like underneath it. I feel this jolt of amazement when I realize that I'm going to get to put my mouth all over him—wherever I want—in just a few minutes.

I'm leaning against the door to my room, and my back is cold against the metal. It's a nice contrast to the warmth of Caleb's body, so close to mine. His hands are pressed against the door, anchored just above my shoulders. He's leaning into me, teasing me, and I'm loving every minute of it.

He moves in, and I can feel the rise and fall of his chest as he's breathing. I wish he would just kiss me already. I go up on my tiptoes to end this torture myself, but I stop short when Caleb slides one of his hands across my shoulder, then up along the column of my neck, until it comes to rest on my cheek. I close my eyes and lean into it, completely under his spell.

"You don't live in the city," he says, his eyes sober despite the clear desire that's written all over his face.

"I just moved here," I tell him. It's not really a lie, so much as it's not the whole truth. It's a temporary move, not a permanent one. "Do you have a room here, or were you just hanging out in the bar, trolling for women?"

Caleb laughs. "I don't have to troll for women, Mia," he replies confidently, sliding his thumb across my cheekbone. "I have a room here. It's on another floor."

"Which floor?" I ask.

"A higher one."

I get the feeling that he doesn't want to be a jerk and tell me that he's staying in the penthouse, but my stomach sinks at the realization that he has a room here too. That means-

"So, you don't live here in the city, either?"

"I just had some work done on my apartment," he says, smiling. "A friend of mine owns the hotel, so he offered me a place to stay while the work was being completed."

"*Was* being completed?" Was means that he's leaving. Soon.

"I'm checking out tomorrow."

I take a deep breath. "Oh." Seems like I'm working on even

more borrowed time than I thought I was, and I don't intend on wasting another second of it. I twist myself out from under his arms, and slide my key card into its slot.

"What are you doing?" Caleb asks, amused.

"I'm opening the door, so we can go inside?" I'm confused. Did I read this wrong? No, that's not possible, because he basically told me that he wanted to have sex with me when we were down in the bar. A quick mental replay of the events since then don't make me feel like I've done anything that would change his mind, so I have no idea why I'm hesitating now.

"I'm not going in there," he says. He's still smiling though, so whatever news is coming next can't be all that bad.

"You're not?"

Caleb reaches up and gently swipes across the crease between my eyebrows, until my face relaxes completely. "No," he says. "I'm not. I want to, don't get me wrong. There's nothing I want more than that. But there's also something I want more than that."

I'm sure that crease appears between my brows again, because what does that mean?

"I'm crazy for this," he says, letting out a little breath as he looks down. He almost seems…bashful. "I know this is probably confusing, and I don't want to confuse you. I didn't go into that bar tonight for a one-night stand, or a quick fuck in a hotel room. I used to be that guy, and I've worked incredibly hard not to be him anymore. I'm trying to do things differently now, and-"

"So you don't want-"

"No," he says firmly. "I very, *very* much do."

"I don't understand," I tell him, honestly. "Is this it?"

"No. *No*," he says, sliding his fingertips along the shoulder of my dress, making me shiver. "This is far from *it*." He licks his lips as he waits for my reaction.

"Then what…I thought that if a man was interested, he didn't, you know, let you get away or whatever."

Caleb wraps his arm around my waist, and pulls me flush against him. His erection is hard against my belly, and he's been such a confusing jackass the past couple of minutes that I move a little, just to torture him.

"I'm interested," he says, his voice choked. "And I'm not letting you get away."

"I can feel that. So what are you proposing?"

Caleb leans forward, and licks his full, pink lips.

"You and me. Dinner tomorrow."

A spark of panic works its way through my lust-filled brain. This guy has money, and dinner with him most likely means going to a nice restaurant. Going to a nice restaurant requires a dress, and I'm wearing the only one that I brought with me. I don't exactly have room in my budget for a new one, especially when I would have to go shopping for it in Manhattan, of all places.

"Um…"

"Something casual," he says quickly. "Just the two of us?"

"Casual?" I ask hopefully.

"Yes. Just you and me spending some time together."

Okay, sure. Yes. I can do that. "I'd like that."

"So," he says, letting his gaze drift down to my lips, and further down towards my neckline. "It's a date?"

I bite my lip to keep myself from grinning like an idiot, but it's too late. "Yeah, it's a date."

"I'll pick you up here?"

"At the bar," I say quickly. I've got to check out of this room tomorrow because I can't afford it anymore, but I don't want to tell him that right now.

His eyebrows draw together, but he doesn't question me. "Okay. Same time?"

I nod, running my hand down his lapel again. Seriously, his muscles. The suit. It's such a good combination. "Same time."

"Goodnight, Mia," he says, as he pulls away. I manage to catch his wrist before he gets too far.

When he turns around, he quirks his eyebrow at me, totally amused. He was expecting me to stop him, and he knows what I'm going to ask.

"You aren't going to kiss me?"

He leans in, until his lips are so close to mine, and all I can see, smell, and hear is *him*. He slides the pad of his thumb across my bottom lip.

"Oh, I'm going to kiss you. You'll be *begging* me to kiss you." For a second, I think he's going to brush his lips against mine. I feel maybe the smallest hint of them. "Soon. But not tonight."

I groan, and let the back of my head thump against the door. This man is going to be the death of me. "Soon," I repeat.

With a wicked grin, Caleb says, "I'll make it worth the wait."

CHAPTER *Four*

My grandmother always told me that a watched pot never boils, which is true in my experience.

I can also attest to the fact that watched location searches never complete. Anxiously waiting on the edge of your seat to hear a dreadful 'ping' doesn't make anything move any faster, no matter how much I wish it was so.

My laptop is sitting on the desk in the corner of my hotel room, cycling through the program that I've written to detect Andre Privya's movement. It's not entirely on the up and up, but this desperate woman is willing to employ desperate measures. It searches hits on credit cards with his name, and the location of the cell phone numbers that I managed to find for him. It's not a foolproof method of figuring out whether or not he's successfully tracking me down, but it's better than nothing. If he goes anywhere while his cell phone is on, and uses a credit card to get there, I'll know about it.

I try desperately not to think about what would happen if he uses cash and travels with a burner phone. Like I did.

On the middle of the bed, sitting with my legs crossed, I take in the lush surroundings of this hotel room. It was a splurge, one that I absolutely cannot afford. When I got to the city, I was scared out of my mind, and too nervous to go to one of the hotels that I could actually afford, which would include thin walls and a shared bathroom, and me jumping at every single noise outside of my room. I walked into this establishment and offered to pay cash just to rest for a few nights. I feel safe here, and don't want to think about leaving. The only good thing is that when I leave tonight, it will be with Caleb, not alone.

Caleb.

It's nice to know that despite my track record of making terrible decisions, that I'm still capable of making good ones, too. Like deciding to go down to the bar last night? That was an excellent decision. My mind was racing, and I could tell that I was on the verge of a panic attack, so I thought I'd slip on the one dress I managed to bring with me when I left Chicago, go down and have a drink to take the edge off. For a couple of hours, I wanted to pretend I was a person who didn't have a care in the world. Fake it till you make it, right?

It worked.

Last night, I felt like myself again. I've only been running for four days, but they've been the four longest days of my life. It's kind of amazing how easy it is to forget all about yourself when you're in the middle of an incredibly stressful situation.

Then Caleb showed up, and I felt like *me*: twenty-three year-old Mia Briggs, computer programming phenom from Chicago, who is a capable, smart woman. Caleb made me feel wanted and sexy, two things I haven't felt in a very long time. Of course, after our conversation in the bar, I thought we were headed for a one-night stand. He threw me for a loop when he didn't even try to kiss me, but the thought that he wants more than just a quick fuck, well...that turned me on enough to make up for it. Which is a little strange, considering I'm not sure that I can give him what he's looking for.

Actually, I am sure. I *can't* give him what he's looking for.

Caleb is a nice distraction, though, and maybe a distraction is just what I need. I'm an intelligent woman, I don't have any doubts about that, but I'm having a hard time figuring out how to get myself out of this situation. In the past, whenever I was stuck on a programming issue, I'd spend a day at the movies, or hang out with a friend.

Now, everyone that I know is in a city that's 800 miles away, under the impression that I was a last-minute addition to a big-time software programming contract with a company in London. These people are more than acquaintances, but I'm not particularly close with them. I know for sure some of them would question me just up and disappearing one day, so

I concocted a cover story, just to be safe. Keeping them in the dark is the best way to protect everyone who knows me, even a little. I don't think Privya would go to them looking for me, but better safe than sorry. If he does, and someone lets it slip that I'm in London, well…that's another false trail for him to follow that will buy me more time here in New York.

There's only one person in Chicago who knows even a little bit about what's going on, and it's time for me to give him a call. I reach into my pocket, and pull out the untraceable burner phone I brought with me. My fingers tremble as I dial his number.

"Hello?"

"Marcus, it's me." I'm speaking quietly for some reason, as if I'm worried about anyone on the other end somehow overhearing my voice.

Marcus lets out a long, audible sigh. "I've been worried about you," he says. "Where are you?"

I pull a pillow onto my lap, and run my fingertip along the seam. "I think it's probably better if I don't say."

"Okay, yeah. That's a good idea." There's a long pause before he says, "Everything is okay here. Nothing out of the ordinary."

Relief washes over me, like I've been doused with a bucket full of it. Just that small bit of news makes me feel better. "Thanks for letting me know."

"No problem."

Marcus and I have been best friends since we were kids,

and we've never had a stilted conversation like this. It feels wrong. Off. Like everything in the world has shifted ten inches to the right, but I'm still standing firmly in place. "How's your mom?"

"She's better. We're moving her into her new facility next week."

I take a deep breath, and fight back the tears that are pricking at my eyes. "Good, I'm glad."

"I wish you would've let me come with you."

"No, my name is the only one attached to this," I remind him. "At least you're safe, and you can let me know what's going on there."

"How am I supposed to do that? I don't even have a number I can reach you on!" Marcus says, his voice louder than it probably should be.

"I'll call you in a day or two," I tell him, trying to calm him down. "It'll be okay."

"And if it's not? What if I don't hear from you? What am I supposed to do then?"

I take a deep breath, because I don't like thinking about that possibility. "Then I guess it turns out that coming here wasn't so clever after all," I say, trying to lighten the situation. I can't have Marcus panicking too, I'm doing that enough for the both of us.

"Mia," he says quietly, and I know what's coming next. "Return the money, hide it as an accounting error or something.

You can do that, can't you? We'll think of something else."

"We've been trying to think of something else for months, Marcus. Time was running out, and I had to do something, okay? It's not like he didn't deserve it." This is what I tell myself to not crumple up in shame and embarrassment at what I've done. "He deserves that and more for what he did to my dad, and to your mom. He's the reason she's in that facility; the least he can do is pay for it. It's going to happen to someone else, and-"

"Mia," Marcus says softly. "Thank you. I never told you that, and I should've."

The tone of his voice, and the complete lack of judgment makes the tears prick behind my eyes. It would be nice to have him here with me; part of me wishes that I had taken him up on the offer, but there's no sense in two of us getting mixed up in this when I can take the fall on my own.

"You don't have to thank me," I tell him. "She always treated me like I was her own. It's the least I could do."

There's silence on the other end of the line, and I get the feeling that Marcus is fighting off the tears like I am. It makes the situation feel even more hopeless, but it also steels my resolve.

"I better go," I tell him.

"Okay."

"I'll call you soon."

I hope with everything I have in me that I can keep that promise.

CHAPTER *Five*

The bar is busier than it was last night, and is chock full of gorgeous men in suits. Any other night, at any other time in my life, I'd be in heaven in a room full of men who look like this. Handsome, in well-tailored suits, talking shop with each other as they decompress from their workdays with drinks in their hands. Tonight, though, I'm only looking for one handsome guy.

I stand just inside the entrance, right behind a pillar, in an area that gives me a good vantage point of the room. I'm short—I can barely clear shoulder height of most of these men—so I'm having difficulty seeing through the crowd. I don't know much about Caleb, but he seems like the kind of guy who would arrive early, just so I wouldn't have to wait.

It only takes me a minute to find him. He's sitting at the same table he found me at last night. I'm not sure why it didn't occur to me to look there first, but finding him there lets me know that he's not only punctual, but he's probably a tad sentimental as well.

I'm pleased to find out that when Caleb said tonight would be casual, he meant it. He's wearing a simple enough outfit, the kind of thing that I normally wouldn't look at twice, but on him, it's a mouthwatering combination: dark jeans and an emerald green henley that shows off the broad expanse of his muscular chest. The collar of the white t-shirt he's wearing underneath peeks out, contrasting nicely against his tanned skin.

I thought the suit he had on yesterday was flattering to his build, but that was nothing compared to this.

My bag is slung over my shoulder, and I grip the handles tightly as I navigate my way through the clusters of people talking. The second that Caleb sees me, his whole face lights up.

"Hi," we both say at the same time.

We repeat it again, and laugh at each other.

It feels so good to be here with him that, operating on instinct, I lean in and press a gentle kiss to his smiling lips. It's nice, and soft, and perfect. When I pull away, my eyes are wide with surprise. I can't believe I did that. Apparently, neither can Caleb.

"I'm sorry, I guess I just-"

Before I have a chance to finish my sentence, Caleb's warm

hands are cupping my face and pulling me in for another kiss. I open my mouth to him, loving the long languid kisses and the feeling of his velvet tongue against mine. I nip at his lip, and his hips buck against me. I want more of this; I don't even care about the world outside of the two of us as long as I get so much *more* of this.

"Don't apologize for that," he says, after he pulls away. His eyelids are heavy with lust, and his chest heaves as he tries to catch his breath. "Don't ever apologize for doing that."

I lean in for more, and Caleb indulges me, until someone beside us coughs loudly. I had completely forgotten we were in public.

When we part, I lick my lips, and slide the pad of my thumb across Caleb's lower lip to wipe off the smear of my lipstick there. We both look at each other, panting a little. After last night, I wasn't sure how our first kiss would happen, but now that I know what it feels like to kiss Caleb? He was right: I would've begged him to do it.

Now, though, I get the feeling that I won't have to beg for anything at all.

"Do you want to get a drink before we go?" Caleb asks. His voice is a little husky, and the fact that I have that kind of effect on someone like him makes me feel powerful.

"Where exactly are we going?"

Caleb grins. "Does your answer hinge on my answer?"

"Perhaps," I say with a coy smile. "If you tell me we're

going to do some kind of trendy date activity, like…I don't know, couples trapeze or something, then my answer is yes. I want to get a drink before we go."

Laughing, Caleb says, "So, drunk trapeze work is something you're interested in?"

"Not drunk, necessarily. Tipsy," I clarify. "Tipsy trapeze work."

Caleb slides his hand down my arm, until his hand clasps mine, leaving goosebumps in its wake. "We're not doing anything circus related. It's very tame."

"Describe 'tame,'" I reply, arching my brow.

"Going to my apartment. Just you and me. It might not stay tame, but it'll start out that way." There is a mischievous kind of promise in his voice that sends a shiver of anticipation along my spine.

"Do you have wine?" Wine is an absolute must.

"Plenty," he replies, pulling me closer. "You can take your pick; anything you want."

"You're not going to tell me that you have a wine cellar, are you?" I say, teasing.

"Not here in the city." He gives me a wry grin. "But I do have one."

I roll my eyes at him good-naturedly. I don't have much experience dealing with the mega-rich, or even the rich, for that matter, but I get the feeling that the best way to deal with anything that shows off their enormous wealth is to just laugh it off. I'm sure Caleb has people fawning all over him for his wealth every day, and I don't want to be that person. I don't care about it, anyway. He could live in a box as long as he keeps kissing me like he just did.

"Are you bringing that with you?" he asks, gesturing toward my huge bag that I've got slung over my shoulder. I know he's curious about why I'm carrying it around.

What can I tell him? That inside the bag is everything I managed to grab from my apartment before I went on the run, because some criminal for hire is after me for bilking an underhanded, awful, scummy man? I don't think a confession like that would make the kissing all that more frequent, and I like the distraction that being around Caleb gives me. I can't seem to come up with a way out of this mess, so I might as well take whatever pleasure I can wherever I can.

I only have enough money to stay in New York for another month or so, and then I'm going to have to...I don't know. Go home and face the consequences for what I've done? Ask for mercy? I don't want to think about that right now.

So, I settle for the truth. "Yeah, I'm switching hotels. I haven't had a chance to check into the new one yet, so I thought I'd just bring this with me. Unless you'd rather I didn't?" I know how it looks; like I'm poised and ready to move in with him. I haven't checked into my new hotel yet; I didn't want to waste the money on a place if I don't wind up staying there tonight.

"No, no," he says quickly. "It just looks heavy, and a little too big for you to carry. Let me?"

Caleb holds out his hand to take it, and I debate about whether or not to let him carry the bag. I'm not sure where the hesitance is coming from. I know in my bones he's not working for Privya, and it's not like he's going to run off with it. I'm getting ready to leave this bar to go with him to his apartment, where no one will be around. If I can't trust him to carry my bag, how in the hell am I going home with him?

I let the bag's strap slide down my shoulder, and then hand it to Caleb. He grips it tightly, and slings it behind his back in a move that I find ridiculously sexy. My heart is pounding in my chest. It's just a bag, but it's my *everything* right now, and for the first time this trip, it's out of my possession.

I take a deep breath. It's going to be okay.

"C'mon," Caleb says, twining his fingers through mine. Immediately, I relax into his touch. He leads me through the crowd, and out onto the street. I feel anxious and exposed, and it seems like Caleb notices, because he gently squeezes my hand, before he looks back and smiles. "My car is right over here."

CHAPTER *Six*

Caleb paints an almost GQ-level picture from where he stands, his hands planted on the sparkling clean gray granite countertop that covers the island in the middle of his kitchen. The place is pristine, and beautiful. It has dark cherry cupboards, and spotless stainless steel appliances. Without asking, I know this is one of the rooms he recently had remodeled.

"Do you like it?" he asks.

I give him a puzzled look, which makes him smile.

"The wine, Mia," he replies, letting out a huff of a laugh. "Do you like the wine?"

Oh. The wine. I had gotten so distracted appreciating the view that I completely forgot there is a glass of superb wine sitting in front of me.

"It's delicious," I tell him, before taking another sip of my red, which came from a bottle that is older than I am. "You said you had the best, and you most definitely have the best."

Glass in hand, I walk around the kitchen, marveling at the thought that was put into the design. Back home in Chicago, my tiny apartment has a galley style kitchen, and it's so cramped that when I open the oven door, it buts into a cabinet. This place doesn't have that issue. I could do cartwheels in here if I wanted to.

"Is this place always this neat?" I ask. "Or is it super pristine because you just had it renovated?"

"Are you asking if I'm a slob?" He doesn't seem offended, even though he probably should be.

"No," I say, shaking my head. "Okay, yes. Maybe a little."

"I have a cleaning lady, if that's what you were wondering," he replies with a smile.

"I'm not judging, by the way. I was just trying to figure out how impressed with you I should be."

"You should be impressed, but not by my cleaning skills." He winks at me, and I think I feel my knees starting to give out.

"What skills should I be impressed by, then?" I ask, coyly looking at him over the rim of my wine glass.

"You'll find out later."

Yep, knees are definitely weak. I need to get some distance from him, because I want to find out all about those skills. Right now.

"Is it okay if I look around?" I ask. I only got a good look at the foyer before Caleb brought me into the kitchen so I could pick out a bottle of wine, and I'm curious about what the rest of the place looks like. I don't want to be rude and go off and explore without asking.

"Absolutely. Let me know what you think."

I walk out of the kitchen, and...wow. This is a *nice* apartment. It has that new construction smell, too, like sawdust and paint.

It's a loft with exposed ductwork on the raised ceiling, and the wall on the far lefthand side is nothing but brick. The apartment somehow manages to be both industrial looking, and warm. Inviting. There is neutral-toned furniture in the living room, surrounding a big-screen television. On the mantel, there are pictures in frames of all shapes and sizes. Many of them feature Caleb with two of the same guys. He must be incredibly close to these people, considering how many pictures they're in together, and how many years the pictures seem to span. There are photos of what looks like Caleb as a child, with a man and a woman that I assume are his parents, although they aren't in any recent pictures.

I understand what that means, and it makes my heart ache. Either he's estranged from his mother and father, or they're dead.

I want to ask Caleb the stories behind these pictures, find out when and where they were taken. I've only just met him though, and I can't expect him to be open and honest about his past and his present, when there's no way I can be open and honest about mine. If he wants me to know who these people are to him, he'll tell me.

When I make my way over to the dining room, I run my finger along the tops of the high-backed chairs. They're upholstered and comfortable-looking, in sharp contrast to the large, imposing table. There is an interesting light fixture hanging from the ceiling—which is lower than the one throughout the rest of the loft—it looks like a chandelier, but is made out of what looks like delicately cut steel pieces. There aren't any personal touches in here, not like in the living room, just a few modern accents hanging on the walls.

"So?" Caleb asks, startling me out of my thoughts.

"It's nice," I tell him. "To be honest, it's not what I was expecting when you invited me over here."

"No? What were you expecting?"

I look around, and shrug. "I'm not really sure how to say this, but I was expecting something more…I don't know, plain? Smaller? This," I say, waving my hand toward the floor-to-ceiling view overlooking Central Park. "This is real estate porn."

"Porn, huh?" Caleb's got this lascivious grin on his handsome face that makes my cheeks flush.

"Yeah," I reply, trying to make it sound like I didn't just bring up *porn*, even if it is of the real estate variety. "The good kind. The classy kind."

Caleb lets out a bark of a laugh, as he walks into the kitchen and picks up his wine glass from the island. I've still got mine in my hand. "Feel like taking a look at the view?"

The thought of walking out on the balcony makes me uneasy. I've never been such a fan of heights, and we're up high. *Really, obscenely* high.

"Don't worry," Caleb says, sliding the stems of our glasses between his fingers, before reaching out for my hand. "I won't let you fall."

Falling seems like it would be so easy around him, but I feel safe here with him.

Our fingers twine together, and he leads me out onto the patio.

After being in New York for a few days, cooped up in a hotel room, I've nearly forgotten what fresh air feels like. Caleb and I are so far away from street level that the air seems different up here. Cleaner, cooler. I take long, deep breaths, filling my lungs with it.

We're both leaning against the railing, taking in the quiet calmness of the expansive park below. Our elbows are touching, and heat from just that small point spreads all throughout my body. I take a subtle step to my right, trying to get closer to Caleb, hoping I'm not too obvious about it. My fear of heights isn't really bothering me right now, probably because the patio is huge, and there are thick, cement railings all around us. And, cheesy as it sounds, I feel safe standing out here with Caleb next to me.

"Is it okay if I ask what you do for a living?"

This is a question I can answer without any hesitation. "I'm a software designer."

"Wow," he replies, clearly impressed. "How did you get into that?"

I shrug. "It's always been something that I've been interested in. I think it's awesome that we have the ability to write code that can make a computer do pretty much anything you need it to do. Within reason, of course. And sometimes outside of it. When I was a kid, my dad and I lived next door to this older gentleman—Mister DiGrazia—and he used to let me play with all of his spare Commodore machines. It was love at first sight."

Caleb laughs, and in the ambient light shining outside from his apartment, I can see him smiling at me.

"I can turn my laptop on, and check my email. That's… yeah, that's pretty much the extent of it."

"I like learning how things work. The ultimate way to do that is to make it yourself, so that's what I do."

"Do you have your own company?" he asks, before taking a sip of his wine.

"No," I reply, oddly flattered that he thinks that I would.

"It's more like I'm a contractor, and I'm my own boss."

Caleb gives me a fond smile that's so bright I wan to bask in it.

"What do you do?"

He takes a deep breath, and lets it out slowly. "I've got my hands in a lot of jars," he says, grinning. "It would've driven my father crazy. For the most part, I suppose you could say I'm a venture capitalist." He cringes when he says the words, like he's waiting for some kind of judgment from me. Far be it from me to judge anyone for anything right now, so I just nod my head, encouraging him to go on.

"What other jars are your hands in?"

"Business consulting. Mainly for two guys that I've known since I was a kid, Ben and Oliver, but I do take on other work from time to time."

Looking out over the park, I close my eyes as a cool spring breeze blows through my hair. "Which one of them owns the hotel?"

"That would be Oliver," he says. "He owns a few boutique hotel chains in New York."

"The city or the state?" I tease.

"Both. He's looking to expand, but it's taking some time. He drags his feet about pretty much everything. I'm going to have to send him a thank you note, by the way. For offering me that room while this renovation was being completed."

His eyes are shining in the moonlight, and he looks so

irresistible when he says the right things. It would be ridiculous if I actually swooned, so I manage to control myself. I do lean in and give him a soft, quick, chaste kiss. Mainly because I have to put my lips on his right now, but I'm not ready to take things further. Yet.

"And Ben? What does he do?"

"He owns a software company." Caleb's eyes widen so quickly that I can practically see an animated light bulb pop up in a thought bubble over his head.

"No," I say, because I already know what he's thinking.

"Maybe he has some work you can help him with."

I shake my head. I don't even need work right now, especially not working with a new client who will want to look into my references. I have a few projects I can work on from here, with businesses that already know and trust me. I'm having a difficult time getting that work done as it is.

"You haven't even seen what kind of work I can *do*, Caleb. For all you know, I'm terrible. I mean, my work is excellent, but don't go recommending me to him based on…" I wave my hand between us. "Whatever this is."

He looks almost crestfallen at my answer, and I feel like a terrible person for shooting him down right away. He knows that I'm new in town, and for all he knows, I need to make some business contacts. It was very generous of him to even think of recommending me to his friend, but I absolutely cannot take him up on that offer, even if I was planning on staying in town.

"Thank you, though," I say, sliding my hand down his forearm. "It was very sweet of you to think of me, but I don't want to start having anything handed to me, okay?" Not to mention the fact that I don't want to get involved in anything that will make it difficult for me to leave town. I'm already treading dangerous water where that's concerned. I came here to hide out, not make connections. And yet here I am…

"I understand." He gives me a smile that lets me know that's the absolute truth.

"Thank you."

"So," Caleb says, looking down at his glass before his eyes meet mine again. "You said you're new in town. What brought you here?"

Shit.

Of course he would ask the one question that I absolutely do not want to answer. I hate being the kind of person who skates around telling the truth using technicalities, but I'm going to be that person tonight. I don't want to lie to him, but I also don't want him to look at me like I know he will if I tell him the truth. If I tell him the truth, this ends right here. Right now. I'm sure of it.

Maybe it's selfish, but I don't want that. I want to make this last for as long as it can.

"I was looking for a fresh start in a place where I didn't know anyone, and no one knew me. I just…I really needed to get out of Chicago."

Caleb looks at me with this intense gaze, like everything in him is focused directly on me, and he can see my deepest, darkest secrets. "I understand needing a fresh start."

"Yeah?"

He nods. "Yeah. I don't want to assume anything, so I can only speak from my own experience, but sometimes being in a place where you're constantly reminded of what happened there, or what used to be...it's not good for you."

Even though I'm not sure where this piece of information fits in the puzzle that is Caleb, he's showing me a part of himself. He's laying it bare for me to examine, and I feel like it's only right for me to do the same thing. I'm feeling incredibly vulnerable tonight, and I don't want to let anything slip that I shouldn't, but I can share something with him. Don't I at least owe him that?"

"My childhood home, it was in this crappy, low-income building, but I had good memories there," I tell him. "It burned down last year, and...I couldn't even go on that side of town anymore. I'd pass it all the time when I was riding the El, and it made my breath catch every time. There was this hollow ache in my stomach that didn't ease up until I left."

I don't tell him that my father was still living in that building when it burned down. I don't tell him-

"It's nice to go to a place where you don't run into a memory every time you turn around."

I nod, then move closer to Caleb, and this time I don't try to hide it. He wraps his arm around me, and I snuggle into his warmth. With my head buried against his neck, I breathe in the clean smell of him, then press my lips against his neck. He lets out this low rumble that barely even registers, but I can feel it against my cheek, and then we're kissing.

It's soft, and long, and slow, and makes the kiss that we had earlier in the bar almost tame in comparison. Our tongues brush together, and Caleb's fingers tangle in my hair, pulling me closer. I wrap his henley around my fingers, grabbing a fistful of fabric, just needing something to hold onto.

When we stop and take a time out to breathe, he says, "Let's go inside."

CHAPTER Seven

"C'mere," Caleb says, crooking his finger at me.

He's sitting on the couch, relaxing back into the cushions, with a lust-drunk look on his face. We haven't had that much wine, but he's clearly got a little bit of a buzz going. The whole effect on him is really nice.

I take a step into the space between Caleb's knees, and he gives me this cute pout in return. Clearly he was expecting me to move in a way that provided us with a lot more body-to-body contact. Intent on achieving this, he takes my hand and gives it a little tug.

"*C'mere,*" he says again, more emphatically this time, inviting me onto his lap.

With the soft lilt of Caleb's voice and the desire in his eyes, I can't say no to that. I lower myself down until I'm straddling him, my knees planted on either side of his thighs. One of his hands comes to rest on my hip, and the other slides around to the small of my back, where his fingertips find their way beneath the hem of my shirt. His palm presses against my skin, and I move, giving us a little bit of friction. It's not too much, and we're both wearing jeans, but still…it's good.

I sink further down, until I can feel his erection, and I move my hips again. Caleb sucks a breath through his teeth in a long, quiet hiss.

"Mia," he breathes.

Our lips crash together in a heated frenzy, and Caleb licks into my mouth. He tastes sweet, like the wine, and his lips are warm and insistent. The hand that was resting on my back slides across my hip to run up my side, lifting my shirt up as he goes. What I want is for him to take my shirt off, to touch me without fabric between us, but he doesn't seem to want to do that just yet.

"Are you teasing me?" I ask, breathless.

I feel Caleb smiling against my mouth. "Mmm. Yes," he replies. "And I'm teasing myself, too."

My hands slip down his chest, across the broad, rippling muscles that are hidden beneath his henley. When I reach the waist of his jeans, I scoot back on his lap a little to give myself better access.

"What are you-"

I cup him through a layer of denim, pressing my palm against his cock as I glide my hand back and forth. There's this soft, barely-there whimper that escapes the back of his throat as he rocks up against me, enjoying the friction. The fact that I can make a noise like that come from a man like Caleb, gives me a sense of power that swirls in with the lust that's coursing through my veins. Caleb's head drops to the crook of my neck as he lets himself get lost in sensation. He starts sucking on my neck, then he plants soft, teasing kisses along the neckline of my shirt.

It's…it's too much. It's also nowhere near enough.

"Take it off," I breathe.

"Yeah?" Caleb says, his lips against my ear. "Why should I?"

A short, quiet whine escapes my lips before I can stop it, and I can feel Caleb's smile. "Because," I say, panting. "Because…"

"Tell me what you want, Mia. Or else you won't get it."

"I want…" His hands and lips are doing things to me, making it difficult for me to *think.*

"Say it."

"I want your hands on me. I want to feel your mouth on me."

Slowly, so *slowly*, Caleb slides my shirt up and over my head. He takes a moment and gives me an appreciative look, then he gives me exactly what I asked for: his hands on me. His mouth on me.

His fingertips tease the clasp of my bra, while he kisses a

trail across the lacy cup covering my right breast, then my left. He gently bites my nipple through the fabric, his warm breath giving me goosebumps. When he undoes my bra, I can't help but shrug out of it as quickly as possible, letting it fall to the floor.

Caleb immediately palms my breasts, and my head falls back as I let out a moan, reeling from the pleasure of his touch. I have to clasp my hands around his wrists to steady myself; it would be so easy to lose myself in his touch. His hands are rough in a good, *good* way. He flicks his thumbs across my nipples, and then leans in and teases me with his tongue. He sucks my left nipple into his mouth, his soft, warm tongue rubbing across it, driving me crazy.

I want to give him as much pleasure as he's giving me, so I unbutton and unzip his pants. Caleb's so worked up over what he's doing that he doesn't seem to notice that I've got plans of my own until my hand slips under the waistband of his boxer briefs, and around his thick, hard cock.

As I stroke him, Caleb leans back, watching my hand move up and down his length. He's still cupping my breasts, still working my nipples, and it feels so good. It feels even better, watching him watching me touch him like this.

I slide my thumb over the bead of moisture that has formed on the head of his cock, and I can actually feel him shudder. He kisses me then, all lust-drunk and sloppy, and it's *so* good. He pulls away after nipping my bottom lip, and in a move I'm incredibly grateful for, he flips me until I'm spread out on the sofa, and he's kneeling on the floor between my legs.

Caleb wastes no time unbuttoning my pants. A little earlier in the evening, I would've expected him to be all about teasing and seduction, but we're well past that point now. The two of us are nothing but fiery lust and need at this point. He curls his fingers around the waist of my pants and my panties, and slides them down quickly. He tosses them somewhere over his shoulder—I barely even register it—and then sits back for a moment, just looking at me. I'm spread open before him, with nothing between us now. He's still fully dressed, aside from his pants hanging off of his waist, and being naked here in front of him like that turns me on even more.

He runs his hands up the insides of my thighs, then licks his lips in anticipation.

"I'm going to make *you* feel as good as you made *me* feel," he says, his voice dripping with lust and promise. "And I'm not gonna stop until you're so exhausted you can't keep your eyes open. How does that sound?"

I look down at him, and can barely focus on anything that isn't his warm breath against my skin, and how close his mouth is to the place I want him more than anything.

"Mia," he says, sliding his hands up, up, up, until his thumbs are rubbing maddening circles oh-so-close to my clit. "How does that sound?"

I lick my lips and let out a long breath. Caleb's looking

right at my mouth, like he wants to kiss me senseless.

"It sounds good," I reply. Short, simple words are all I can manage at this point.

Caleb leans forward, and slides the flat of his tongue across my wet slit, circling my clit before sucking it into his mouth.

"Oh god," I cry, gripping his hair between my fingers.

Caleb's arms crook under my knees, then he grips my hips, and pulls me down so my ass is resting right on the edge of the sofa. The look in his eyes is nearly predatory, and his lips are wet from me.

"It sounds *good*?" he asks, trying to sound offended. Then, as if he wants to prove some kind of a point, he goes down on me with reckless abandon. He's licking and sucking at a maddening pace, and I'm rocking my hips against his face, wanting any kind of friction it will give me. I can't even hang on to him anymore, I'm just a writhing mess, desperate to come. I grip the back of the couch for leverage, for something that tethers me to this world.

Caleb slips his fingers inside of me, and I'm done for. Breathless, muscles squeezing him, pleasure coursing across every nerve in my body as I cry out. He holds onto me as I ride out my orgasm, and when my breathing finally slows, I grip his henley and pull him up for a kiss. He tastes like me, and I moan into his mouth.

"Still sound good?" he asks, grinning.

"It sounds great," I reply between kisses. "It sounds

amazing. Mind blowing."

"Mind blowing?"

I nod. My body is firing off aftershocks from my orgasm, so I grind against his cock. His boxers are still down from where I touched him earlier, so it's just skin on wet, slick skin, and I can tell it catches Caleb off guard.

Caleb picks me up, and I wrap my legs around his waist.

"I want you, Mia. I've wanted you since the moment I saw you in that bar."

"I want you," I say, grinding against him again. His patience is obviously wearing thin, and I love that. I want him to lose control.

He leans in, and sucks on the skin just behind my ear before he says, "Don't make me wait."

CHAPTER *Eight*

"You're staring," Caleb says, grinning.

"You're beautiful." My thoughts are kind of a jumbled-up mess as I'm kneeling on the edge of Caleb's bed, drinking in the sight of his naked, perfect body. His skin is tanned and practically flawless, muscles rippling everywhere in an understated way. It's not obnoxious, he just looks…sculpted. His cock is hard and ready; the sight of it makes my mouth water, and my body sings with anticipation. I want him inside of me more than I want anything else right now. I might want it more than I've ever wanted anything, which is just a ridiculous notion.

It still seems true, right here in the moment.

Caleb takes a step toward me, gently sliding his hand across my cheek, until his fingers tangle in the hair at the nape of my neck. We kiss, and as we're kissing, he plants his knee on the bed, bringing his other hand around to the small of my back. He moves forward, taking me along with him, until my head is resting on a soft, fluffy pillow. He kisses me some more, warm and slow, and I slide my hands across every inch of his body I can reach.

When the kisses and touches are no longer enough, Caleb sits back on his knees, and I let out a soft groan at the loss of his heat across my body. His mouth quirks up in a cocky grin as he reaches across me—into his nightstand—for a condom. Just as he starts to open it, I reach up and slide it from between his fingers.

"Let me," I tell him.

He licks his lips as I sit up, my legs spread with him kneeling between them, our arousal firing on all cylinders. I bring the foil packet up to my mouth, catch the edge of it between my teeth, and pull. I can hear the long breath of air Caleb inhales as lean forward and roll the condom down his cock. Once it's on, I stroke him a couple of times, loving the way his body trembles as he keeps a tenuous hold on his control.

I can tell that Caleb is at the end of his rope, hanging on by a single thread, and as much as I like teasing him, I don't want to *torture* him. So, I lie back, and hook my leg around his waist.

"Don't make me wait," I tell him, playfully repeating the words he had used on me earlier.

He growls—actually *growls*—as he plants his hands above

my shoulders, and lowers himself down on top of me.

Starting at Caleb's lips, I kiss my way across his cheek, down the column of his neck, along the curve of his shoulder. I stop and suck little spots here and there, wanting to make sure he sees evidence of this night on his skin long after it's over. Meanwhile, he's teasing me with the head of his cock, pressing it against me, but not entering. He lets it slip up and down my slit, then rubs my clit with it, making me crazy. Crazy enough to beg.

"Please," I whisper, moving my hand to the small of his back and pushing down, hoping I have enough strength to move him forward.

"Please what? I won't do it if you don't ask." He pulls away from me, leaving me wanting in order to drive his point home.

I bite my lip, frustrated, and buck my hips to see if I can find a little friction, but there's nothing.

"Please," I whisper, almost whine. "I want you inside of me. Now."

Caleb lines himself up with my entrance, wearing a wicked, sexy grin. He pushes in just far enough to make me lose my patience.

"Fuck me," I say, breathless as I wrap my legs around his hips.

"My pleasure."

Caleb thrusts, sliding all the way inside of me, and we both let out long, low moans. *Finally.* He's balancing himself on his right elbow, and the fingers on his right hand curl between mine and hold on tight. He latches onto my neck, sucking, and licking, and kissing the tender, heated skin there. Slowly, he drags his left hand across the swell of my breast, and he flicks my nipple before going lower, until his thumb finds my clit.

He rubs it in a rhythm that is opposite to the one he's moving his hips to; it's a slow, steady, *glorious* torture. I squeeze him every time he slides out of me, making him grunt in my ear. It's a sound I could get addicted to, and I'm going to do anything I can to hear it again, and again, and again. I plant my feet on the bed to give myself leverage, and I meet him thrust for thrust.

"Fuck," Caleb whispers, so low I'm not even sure I'm supposed to hear it. "*Fuck*."

When we kiss—desperately—something inside of me starts unraveling, giving in to the pleasure that's pulsing all the way out to my fingertips and toes. I feel Caleb *everywhere*, and we move together in perfect sync, like we were made to make each other feel like this. Caleb pounds into me, and I'm falling, coming with his name on my lips, pressing sloppy kisses against his skin, in every single spot I can reach. He lets me ride out my orgasm, before he props himself up on his elbows and cradles my face in his hands.

"Mia," he says. It's kind of soft, and full of something that I can't quite get a read on.

I reach up and put my hands over his. He leans down and

presses his forehead against mine, his breath warm across my face.

"Let go," I tell him, before I kiss him.

Caleb pumps his hips a few more times, then his whole body stiffens as he cries out. His chest is heaving, and his weight is so warm and welcome. My hands rub a long circuit up and down his back, and when he opens his eyes, looking sated and happy, he smiles.

"Stay," he says.

I do.

CHAPTER *Nine*

I wake up with Caleb's strong, warm arms wrapped around me. My back is pressed tightly against his chest, his face is nuzzled in the crook of my neck. I can feel the scratchy whiskers on his cheek and chin against my skin. He breathes in and out, making my hair flutter against my cheek.

There's a cool, bluish light that's beginning to peek into the room from behind the heavy curtains. It's still very early—barely dawn—but I feel like I've been sleeping for hours. I'm rested. I'm waking up from the most peaceful, restful sleep I can remember having in a long time, even before I left Chicago. That, coupled with the hangover from all the sex Caleb and I had last night, I feel almost euphoric.

My body, though, is thoroughly *exhausted.* Even though I'm lying perfectly still, I can feel the ache between my thighs. I'm not complaining, not at all. It's a good ache, one that makes me smile and shiver when I remember all the things that Caleb and I did that made me feel this way. Rounds two, three, and four hadn't been as hurried and desperate as the first, but they were just as intense. They were focused, and intimate, and memorable.

Caleb is *amazing* in bed. Amazing probably isn't even the right word for it, but it's the only one that pops up in my over-sexed mind at the moment. He's attentive, and giving. Sex with him is probably—no, it's definitely—the best sex I've ever had.

An icy cold chill dampens my buzz, because it's the best sex I've ever had, and...heartbreakingly, I realize, it's only temporary. I absolutely cannot get attached to having this. I can't get used to this feeling, because I'm not going to stay here in New York. Andre Privya is looking for me, *right now*, and he probably has a plan of action, unlike me. Sadness creeps up, washing over me, making me feel heavy and weak.

Caleb isn't some great guy that I've met in a new city, where a world of possibility is waiting at my feet. This thing we have—whatever it is—is on a timer. It has an expiration date. If I'm lucky, I can manage a graceful exit, ease my way out of it with an excuse, or a lie. I can tell him I'm homesick, or that things just aren't working out between us. I can make up some ex-boyfriend that I want to get back together with, and hope he leaves it at that, without asking any questions.

I can hope this thing just fizzles out, instead of exploding. Maybe this was just a one-night thing, and I'm worrying for nothing. Maybe he'll wake up, and I'll pull on the same clothes I wore last night, grab the bag that holds everything I brought to the city with me, and he'll walk me to the door and tell me he had a great time. Maybe that will be it.

I slide my hand across Caleb's arm, and he lets out this sleepy little noise as he pulls me even closer. His erection is pressing against the small of my back, and I want to turn around in his arms and kiss him awake. I want to sling my leg over his waist, and ride him until he cries out my name. I want to make him feel as good as he made me feel last night, into the morning.

Oh, god. What was I thinking? I left Chicago with the sole purpose of finding a safe place where I could plan my way out of the mess I'd gotten into. Here I am, just as clueless about how to do that as I was four days ago, and I walked straight into another mess in the making. I let a handsome face and charming personality make me forget about pretty much everything. It's been nice, not feeling like I'm living on borrowed time, or like everything in the world is about to come crashing down around me. I like being with Caleb.

It's the newness talking, I know this. It's the promise of the honeymoon phase, when everything is perfect and the sex is never-ending, and both of us are still mysteries to each other. This is the time before reality hits, when I don't know what a slob Caleb is, or that he has the habit of putting empty cartons of milk back in the refrigerator, or that he picks his teeth at stoplights.

I know I'm getting ahead of myself. I *know* this. I need to enjoy the here and the now, whether it lasts for another fifteen minutes, or...however long. I just can't shake the feeling that this is good, that I'm safe here with him. I also can't shake the thought of the way I know he'll look at me when I tell him what I did that brought me here in the first place. Foolish as it is, I want to push that moment as far off into the future as possible.

What I need to do is enjoy the feeling of being wrapped in his arms while I have it. I need to feel safe and secure while I can.

So, I close my eyes, and let myself drift.

It's well after 11 a.m. when I open my eyes again. When I wake this time, I've got my head resting on Caleb's chest, and he's running his fingers through my hair.

"Morning," he says, looking down at me. His voice is low and sleepy, and his eyes still have that slightly puffy early morning look, so I know that he hasn't been awake for very long. He's smiling, and that smile is a really nice thing to see first thing when I wake up.

"Good morning," I reply, stretching out as much as I can, considering I'm all wrapped up against Caleb's body. Not that I'm complaining. No, not at all. The move makes me press into his side, and my nipples tighten as they rub against his skin. He cuddles me closer, sliding his arm around the small of my back. If I wasn't so sore, I'm pretty sure I'd be pulling him on top of me right about now. Still, I lean into him, and take a deep breath. The man's smell is like a drug to me.

"How did you sleep?"

"Well," I say, pressing a kiss to his chest. "You?"

"Well." He crooks his finger beneath my chin, then tilts my head up and kisses me. "I'm glad you stayed."

I'm grinning at him like a loon, and I don't care one bit. "I'm glad I stayed, too."

"Last night was…" he takes a deep breath, like he's trying to search for words.

"Amazing." I kiss his chest again. I'm pretty sure this would be one of my favorite places to put my mouth on his body, even if it wasn't the only one I could reach right now.

"Fucking amazing."

"Literally."

Caleb laughs, and pulls me on top of him. My thighs come to rest on either side of his hips, and I wince at the ache I feel when he moves me. It's worth it, though, being in this spot.

"Sore?" he asks, running his hands down the small of my back, and over my ass, stopping when he reaches my thighs.

"Little bit."

"Sorry," he replies. "But I'm not *really* sorry."

He looks so mischievous and sleep-rumpled that I have

to kiss him, morning breath be damned. This kiss is slow, and soft, and makes me want to melt right into him. "I'm not sorry, either. Sex has to be the best reason for aching muscles," I admit. "Best workout ever."

Caleb grins, and nuzzles his nose against my cheek. "If working out made me come like that, I'd be in the gym all the time."

I let out a short little laugh as I trail my fingertip down the ridges between his abs. "You don't look like you're in need of more gym time."

Caleb flips me, and my back is pressed against the mattress. Anchoring his weight on his arms, he lowers himself down until his chest touches mine, and his hard cock rubs against my belly. He gives me a kiss, and then lifts himself back up.

"Did you just…did you just do a sexual push up?" I ask. It's a completely ridiculous, show-off move, but it turns me on like I never would've expected.

He arches his brow. "Maybe."

I slide my fingertips across his shoulders. "Do it again."

He does. This time he stays down longer, kissing me thoroughly. I buck my hips against him, providing some friction as a little reward. Just when I decide that the ache between my thighs isn't going to stop me from having sex with him again, my stomach conspires against me by letting out a loud, embarrassing growl. Of course, Caleb laughs.

"Worked up an appetite, huh?"

I nod. I worked up one hell of an appetite.

"How about some breakfast?"

I give him a skeptical look. "You can cook?"

"No, I'm a total disaster in the kitchen. But I can take you to my favorite place for bacon and eggs."

Bacon and eggs sounds really good, but I turn and look at the clock on the table beside the bed. "It's almost lunch time."

"Then we'll get some fries to go with it."

I sigh, running my hands across his abs. He's so beautiful, and it's just unfair. "You eat like that, and look like this."

After he kisses me, he says, "I can always work it off later."

CHAPTER *Ten*

In a corner of the busy diner, Caleb and I sit across from each other at a cozy little booth. Caleb's legs are so long that our legs are tangled up together, and after spending hours wrapped around each other last night, neither one of us bothers to move. I don't know how Caleb feels about it, but it's nice to keep the connection here in public.

Yet again I'm reminded that this thing is moving way too fast, but—and I know this is incredibly short-sighted and stupid—I don't want to stop it.

"I have to ask you a question," Caleb says, swiping a fry through a puddle of ketchup that's in the middle of the plate we're both sharing.

My heartbeat picks up, and I tamp down the panic that is threatening to rise. "Okay."

"The bag you carry everywhere..."

My breath catches. “Yeah?”

“Do you carry it with you *everywhere*, or is it just because you’re in a new place?” He’s got this charmed smile on his face, so I know that I’m not being interrogated, but at least now I know that he has actually noticed the bag. Not that it’s a difficult thing to notice, considering I’ve had it with me every time I’ve seen him. I had just hoped he hadn’t been paying attention to it.

I look down at the bag, where it’s sitting on the floor beside my feet. Its handles are wrapped round my ankle again, even though the booth we’re sitting in is adjacent to a wall. No one can reach over and take it from me without crawling under the table first, but still…I feel safer with it like this.

“It’s because I’m in a new place. My livelihood is in this bag, so are all the things that I brought with me,” I tell him. It’s a vague explanation, but definitely not a lie. “I don’t feel comfortable leaving it in the hotel when I’m not there.”

“And you feel comfortable carrying it around the streets of New York?” he asks, quirking his eyebrow at me as he steals another fry.

I want to tell him that I feel safe as long as it’s with me, because if I have to run, I won’t have to worry about leaving anything behind if all I’ve got is with me. Instead, I say, “I’ll stop doing it once I’m settled in somewhere.”

“You could’ve left it at my apartment,” he says.

I look down at my plate, at the half-finished bacon and

eggs. "I wasn't sure I'd be going back there."

After the words are out, I look up at Caleb, and catch the moment his entire expression changes. He was all teasing and light a minute ago, but now he just seems crestfallen. He schools the look quickly, but still…I saw it there.

"Oh," he says.

"What I mean is that I wasn't sure you'd invite me back after this, and I didn't want to assume anything in case this was, like, the *end* of things." I'm rambling, and I really don't want to make a big fool of myself here, but I can't seem to help it.

"Mia," Caleb sighs. He's got this soft look in his eyes as he reaches across the table and takes my hand, and my frazzled, overworked nerves calm instantly.

"I don't know what's going on here, I'll be honest with you. But I do know that I want to see you again. This isn't the end of things."

"Okay." I smile.

"Yeah?" he asks, smiling too.

"Yeah."

Our hands are still entwined, so he brings mine up to his lips and kisses my knuckles. I feel the blush creeping up my cheeks, because he manages to make this feel intimate and romantic, even though we're in the middle of a diner.

When he reaches for another fry, I say, "I might have to take that back if you don't leave any for me."

Just to be cocky, he takes another one. "You wouldn't dare."

In what is the first extended awkward moment since we met, Caleb and I stand outside of the diner, facing each other. I know I'm definitely trying to figure out what to say to him, and it seems like he's busy figuring out how to broach the subject of what to do next. I want to go back to his apartment with him, no doubt about it. But what I need to do is go and check into the hotel I was going to check into last night. I want to run another search on Privya, and I don't think I could manage that at Caleb's without him asking me questions.

"Would you like to come back to my apartment with me?"

"I think I should go back to my hotel."

We both speak at the same time, and we both look at each other with wide eyes once we're through, and oh, his face. I reach up and quickly cup his cheek. After the conversation we had over brunch about this being just the beginning of things between us, I don't want him thinking that we're not on the same page.

"I do want to go back to your apartment," I tell him quickly. "It's just that…"

I need a moment to consider how I want to go about saying what I need to say next.

"Just that what?" Caleb asks impatiently.

I swallow. I shouldn't say it, but I'm going to.

"I'm worried that the more time I spend with you, the more difficult it will be for me to leave."

His eyebrows scrunch together. "Where are you going?"

I didn't mean to come off like I'm leaving forever, but I guess honesty sneaks out in the places you least expect it to. "Nowhere, just…I meant leave you, leave your apartment. I'll want to stay all the time, and I don't know if that's a good thing. We *just* met."

"I know," he says, laughing. "But it seems like it's been longer than two days."

"It does," I reply. This is the kind of thing that happens in movies, isn't it? Arriving in a new place and getting swept off their feet. Now I understand the stories I've heard about two people meeting each other in a romantic city, and coming home married after only knowing each other for a couple of weeks. Not that things are going to go that way with Caleb and me.

He kisses me, and wraps his arm around my waist.

"At least let me drive you and your bag back to your hotel," he says with a cute little smile.

"Okay."

The same driver who brought us to Caleb's apartment from the bar is driving us back to my hotel. Caleb and I are quiet for most of the ride. I'm nervous, because I lied to Caleb about which hotel I'm staying in. I'm sure I'll wind up regretting that decision at some point, but what's done is done. I remember Caleb telling me about his friend Oliver, who is in the hotel business. Since Caleb did some consulting work for Oliver, I'm sure he's familiar with the hotels in the city, and I don't want him to know that I'm staying in one of the cheaper ones in Manhattan.

It's the kind of place where the bed will take up the majority of the available square footage, and I'll have to share a bathroom with a few rooms on the same floor. I figured that if I told Caleb about it, he'd either a: want me to stay with him, or b: insisted that I get a room at another establishment. I can't afford anything else, and I don't want him paying for me, so lying was the only thing I could think to do.

When the car comes to a stop about five blocks away from the hotel I'm actually going to check into, Caleb says, "Let me walk you up."

"No!" I reply, too loudly. Too quickly. "If you come up, I'll want you to stay. Let's just say goodbye here?"

Caleb gives me an indulgent smile. "That worried you won't be able to resist my charms?"

He leans in close, and kisses the breath right out of me. It's a kiss that makes me rethink my decision to get out of this car.

"When can I see you again?" he asks, his green eyes half-lidded with desire.

"When do you want to see me again?"

"Right now," he says, leaning in and pressing a kiss against my neck. "Don't leave. Come home with me."

"Caleb…" I intend for it to be a warning, but his name comes out more like a plea.

"Okay, okay," he relents. "Tomorrow?"

Way back in the corner of my mind, I hear my grandmother's voice telling me not to be too available for a man, but I just don't care. I don't know how much time I have left here. How much time I have left at all, really. I want to spend time with Caleb while I can.

"Tomorrow sounds good," I say, smiling. How will I even wait that long?

He reaches into his pocket and pulls out his phone, handing it to me. "Give me your number?"

I bite my lip, and input the number to the untraceable phone I have with me, since it's the only one I've got with me, and it would be stupid to give him my real number anyway. I don't even dare turn that phone on.

When I hand the phone back to him, he presses on the screen, and then my phone starts ringing.

I laugh. "What are you doing?"

"Just checking."

Something in my heart sinks knowing that he thought—for even one second—that I might have given him a fake number. "Caleb," I say, reaching out and sliding my hand across his cheek. He leans into it, like a puppy. "I'm not going to blow you off."

He nods, then kisses me. "I'll call you, okay?"

"I can't wait."

I reluctantly get out of the car, and I can feel his eyes on me as I make my way toward the doors of the hotel that I'm totally lying about staying in. I slip inside and grab a pamphlet from the concierge, pretending like I'm thinking about making a reservation, or booking a party. I slip it into the side pocket on my bag, because I need to remember the name of this place. When or if Caleb asks about it, I can't slip up.

I shake my head. I've never been a liar, and now I'm a liar and a thief. Luckily, I don't have much time to devote to think about that right now. When I'm certain that Caleb's car is long gone, I exit the hotel, and head toward the place I'm really staying tonight.

CHAPTER *Eleven*

"How's your mom? I ask Marcus, speaking in a voice that's as quiet as I can manage. I've been in this hotel for nearly a week now, and it's driving me insane. The walls are paper thin, and I'm worried someone will hear me. Not that any of them would care about who I'm talking to or what I'm talking about, but I can't be too careful. With my luck, the one time I raised my voice on the phone with Marcus, Andre Privya would be walking by my door.

"She's good. Doing better. Her new doctor is amazing."

I smile. "I'm glad to hear it," I tell him. No matter how I feel about the current state of my life, at least I know it wasn't for nothing.

"How are things with you?"

I consider the question. How are things with me? Apart from the whole hiding from a hitman thing, things are great.

I've been spending a lot of time with Caleb, and it's wonderful. When I'm with him, I can almost believe that everything is going to be okay. I can almost believe that I could start a new life here, safely, and just forget about my old one and everything that goes along with it.

"I'm doing well," I tell him, and I'm surprised to realize that it's actually the truth.

I can hear the screen door on the back porch of Marcus's apartment creaking open or shut, I can't tell. I close my eyes, remembering all the time I spent on that porch: me talking him down whenever he broke up with a guy, him convincing me that the guy I was dating wasn't good enough for me. He lives a block away from a pizza shop, and the air always smelled like freshly baked bread and warm, melting cheese. I feel a pang of homesickness just thinking about it.

"No sign of him?" he asks cryptically.

I shake my head, even though I know he can't see me. "No. Still in Chicago, from what I can tell."

"You're not alone, are you? Where you are? Do you…is there someone you can talk to?"

"Yeah," I say with a soft smile, thinking of Caleb. "I have someone to talk to. I'm not alone."

Marcus knows me better than pretty much anyone else in the world, so I'm not surprised when he follows up with, "You met a guy, didn't you?"

I laugh. "Maybe."

"You did," he says accusingly, even though I can hear the laughter in his voice. "You met a guy. Tell me about it."

I bite my lip, then say, "I don't think that's a good idea."

"Yeah. Okay, yeah. I understand."

I hate this distance. I hate that I can't tell Marcus where I am, or what I'm doing. I know he's frustrated by the limitations of our phone calls, and being careful not to give away too much on the off chance that someone is listening. I'm sure he feels no small measure of guilt, since his mother is the reason I set this whole plan into motion. She and Marcus are the ones who are benefiting from this, and I know he feels guilty. He's been my best friend for years, and we've been together through so much: my mom dying, the explosion that killed my father and nearly killed his mom, and now the aftermath of it. Everything is so strained now, and maybe this is how it'll always be. Maybe the weight of what I've done for him and his mom will always hang heavily around our necks, and nothing will ever be the same again.

"Do you think I could just stay?" I ask, because I'm feeling a rare, shining moment of hope that everything will work out for me. "Do you think I could just hide here forever, and start a new life? Do you think he'd get frustrated with looking, and I could just…move on?"

"I don't know, Mia," Marcus replies skeptically. "If you could find a way out of it-"

"There is no way out of it," I tell him. It's the first time

I've voiced the words that I've known deep down in my bones since the moment I left Chicago. "There's no undoing it, there's no pretending I didn't steal a..." I cut myself off, because I absolutely should not say that over the phone, even if I'm fairly certain that no one is listening. I don't want to start getting careless. "Maybe I should just enjoy life while I can and hope for the best?"

"Don't talk like that. I'll go tell him I'm the one-"

I let out a bitter laugh. "Please. He knows it was me, Marcus. There is no sense in getting yourself in trouble when he'll just come after us both, then. We've discussed this before, please don't make me say it again, okay? I need this to not be for nothing. I want to believe that he'll give up, and that I can stay here and...be happy."

"Yeah, maybe he'll give up," Marcus says sadly. I know he doesn't believe that. I don't, either, but it's a nice thought.

It would be a life lived with me constantly looking over my shoulder, and I'd never get to see Marcus again. But the thought of a clean slate is appealing, even though I'd always know what I had done. The prospect of just being happy is a nice one. I haven't felt really, *truly* happy in so long.

"Mia-"

"I should go," I tell him. Caleb is picking me up for dinner in an hour, and I have to get dressed and over to the hotel he thinks I'm staying in before he arrives.

There is a long silence before Marcus finally says, "Okay.

Call me again as soon as you can."

"I will," I tell him, even though I'm not sure it's the truth. "Bye, Marcus."

"Goodbye, Mia."

CHAPTER *Twelve*

On what I'm considering to be our first real date—which I am defining as an outing that does not include dinner and sex at Caleb's apartment—he takes me to an up-and-coming hotspot in TriBeCa. There's a line spilling out the door that stretches all the way down the block, but Caleb's driver lets us out out near the front door, and we walk right up. Caleb doesn't even have to show the host any kind of identification, we just walk right in and pass all of the other people waiting for a table. Inside, a hostess greets Caleb by name, and guides us to our table.

The inside of the restaurant is two stories, but still manages to be very cozy. The whole place is lit with candlelight, and long, white tied-back drapes cordon off different sections of the restaurant, breaking the large space into smaller, more intimate ones.

We're guided to a table in the corner. It's secluded, and I get the feeling that this table is frequently given to Caleb when he eats here.

Caleb slides my chair out for me, and helps me push it back toward the table once I've settled in. Goosebumps cover my skin as his hand glides across my shoulder as he moves to take his seat across from mine.

"They treat you like you own this place," I tell him with a smile.

Caleb shifts in his seat, looking uncomfortable, his eyes focusing on his hands, which are folded on the table.

"Oh my god," I say, stunned. "You *do* own this place."

My eyes go wide, I can't believe it. I look around, and… wow. This is *his*. Not sure why it hits me so hard, or why it shocks me the way that it does.

"It was an investment," he says casually, like restaurants are things that everyone puts money into. I find the blasé way he talks about it to be both charming, and a little maddening.

"I can honestly say that no one has ever taken me to their own restaurant on a date. This is a first."

"Good," he replies, grinning. He looks more relaxed than he did a moment ago. "Firsts are good, especially when they're with me." He gives me a sly little wink as the sommelier comes to the table and pours us some wine. Apparently Caleb had called ahead and asked for it to be decanted. Based on my sampling of the wine collection at Caleb's apartment, I know that he has excellent taste, which means I'm in for a real treat here.

"I hope red is okay?" he says, like he doesn't already know how much I love it. We toast to firsts, and clink our glasses together.

And wow, this red is really, really good.

"So, how does this work?" I ask, noticing that the waiter didn't bring us any menus, and no one has been by to take our order.

"I called ahead and put an order in. I think you'll like what they bring out for us."

"Like it? I'm sure I'll love it." The restaurant smells like heaven; if that's any indication of how the food tastes, 'love' might not be a strong enough word.

I take a sip of my wine, and close my eyes, letting out a soft sigh of satisfaction.

"You look beautiful," Caleb says, reaching under the table and caressing my knee. "I look forward to making you look like that later. More than once," he says, with a playful glint in his eyes.

I feel the flush creep into my cheeks, and look down at my glass.

"Hey," he says softly. "Don't be embarrassed."

When I look up, he's giving me this intense look that makes me glad we're seated away from the crowd. "You're driving me crazy in that dress."

It's the dress I was wearing the night that we met, the one I know that he likes on me. Even if I had something else to wear here tonight, I probably would've chosen this dress anyway.

"Good to know," I reply, smiling.

"You wore that dress on purpose."

"Yes." He doesn't need to know that wearing it was also a necessity.

"I'm going to make you pay for that later," he says. His voice is low and rough, and his eyes are full of promise. "I think you'll like it."

I grin. "I'm sure I will."

"Will you stay with me tonight?" he asks. I desperately want to; it's been a few days since I've had the luxury of falling asleep in his arms. Besides, he talked me into leaving my bag at his apartment, so I have to go back there anyway, and it'll be nice to save the cost of the hotel room for one night.

"I can be persuaded to do that," I tease.

Caleb playfully raises his hand. "Check!"

"Hey!" I say, laughing. "You're not getting out of here that easily. You promised me food, and I expect to get it."

He winks at me and says, "You're going to need your energy for later."

"Mmm," I reply, suppressing a shiver. "I certainly hope so."

Caleb opens his mouth to say something, but something or someone catches his eye. He looks the slightest bit apprehensive as he looks at me, then his gaze flits back somewhere over my shoulder. I'm tempted to turn around, but I don't.

"Mia, my-"

"Caleb?"

"Ben. Hey," Caleb says warmly.

I recognize the name immediately; Ben is the friend of Caleb's who owns the software company - Caleb wanted to recommend my work to him. I look up, and see a familiar face from all the of the pictures on Caleb's mantel. In the photographs I've seen of him, I didn't notice much of a resemblance, but in real life Ben looks a lot like Caleb. He's standing next to a beautiful young woman with curly, dark blonde hair.

"I see you stole my table," Ben says, making Caleb laugh.

"You wish," Caleb replies. His brows scrunch up before he says, "I recall you thinking that this was a bad investment."

"Even a clock is wrong twice a day. Isn't that how the saying goes?"

That is not even remotely close to how the saying goes, and I can't help but laugh. Ben looks down at me, and smiles.

"Felicity," Caleb says, leaning over to hug the woman standing next to Ben. "It's good to see you."

"It's good to see you, too, Caleb."

I'm going to take a wild guess and say that Ben and Felicity are brother and sister.

Caleb finally looks over at me, and his expression

immediately softens. "Mia, this is my friend Ben, and his sister Felicity."

"Ben, Felicity, this is my...Mia."

Felicity's gaze swings over to Caleb, her eyes bright, looking like she's dying to tease him.

Ben doesn't resist the opportunity. "Caleb's Mia, huh?" he says, grinning. "It's a pleasure to meet you."

"You, too," I say, reaching out to shake his hand. I do the same with Felicity.

Caleb looks over at me, like he wants me to give him the okay to invite them to sit down and eat with us. I give him a discreet nod. Much as I was looking forward to having a quiet dinner, just the two of us, I can't help but wonder what I'll find out about Caleb with his friends around.

"Would you like to join us?" Caleb asks.

"Wait," I say, laughing so hard that tears are threatening to spill down my cheeks. "You jumped off the *ski lift*? Because of a *bird*?"

Felicity and Caleb are cracking up, while Ben's all red-faced and looking annoyed, like he's completely done with being teased by his sister and best friend.

"To be fair," he says seriously, "I had been drinking, and I didn't *know* it was a bird. It moved really quickly, and we were almost at the top of the slope, so it's not like I plummeted into a ravine or anything. It's not nearly as funny as Caleb is making it out to be."

Caleb leans over and whispers in my ear, "It was funnier."

I smile at him, loving the demeanor that he has around his friends. There isn't an air of pretense around them; in fact, I feel like I've known Ben and Felicity much longer than I actually have.

"Do you have any crazy spring break stories, Mia?" Felicity asks, as she cuts a piece of her chicken.

Reality slams into me, and I remember that I'm sitting at a table full of people who have probably never wanted for anything in their lives. They're all looking at me expectantly, but there's an anxiousness in Caleb's eyes, like he knows what I'm going to say. I'm desperate to come up with some kind of anecdote, but being put on the spot makes my brain slow down to the point of being useless. It's like being in a hurry to get out of the door and looking for your car keys in a frantic rush, when you were too busy to be able to see that they were right next to your purse the whole time.

"Nothing?" Ben says. "Come on, there's got to be something."

Caleb's warm hand slides down my back, instantly easing my tense muscles. "Ben, she-"

"No spring break stories, I'm afraid," I admit with a smile. "I never actually went on spring break. No, I mean, I went *on* spring break, of course, because school was out and everything.

I just never went on a trip for it." Caleb's hand continues its soothing circuit up and down my spine, and I squeeze his thigh under the table as a silent thank you.

The way Caleb looks at me…yeah, he knew why I hesitated.

Ben and Felicity are looking down at their plates, obviously uncomfortable. I'm desperate to break the tension, and now that there aren't three pairs of eyes trained on me waiting for an answer, I feel like I can breathe.

"I did put my spring break to good use though," I say, and with those words, I can see the tension fall right out of Ben and Felicity's shoulders. "My friends and I would raid their parents' liquor cabinets during the daytime hours, and we'd see who could come up with the best boozy party treats. Mostly we used Easter candy to do it, since it was around that time, and we usually had a ton of it at our disposal."

"What kind of Easter candy?"

I shrug. "Depends on what we were doing. Candy covered chocolate eggs, jelly beans. We'd make Peeps cocktails."

"Peeps cocktails?" Ben asks curiously.

"Yeah, those marshmallow bunnies and birds?"

Ben and Caleb look at each other like they have no clue what I'm talking about. Felicity looks like she's about to bust out laughing.

"Did you guys not have Easter baskets?"

"We did," Ben begins shyly, "but-"

"No Peeps? Oh my god, you guys missed out. Note to self:

find you some Peeps. They weren't so good in the cocktails we made, but they're great if you open the package and let them get stale."

Now everyone at the table is giving me a vaguely horrified look. I can't help but laugh.

"Fine," I say. "More for me, then."

After we are finished with dinner, and working on our second bottle of wine, Ben asks me what I do for a living.

I look over at Caleb and narrow my eyes, because I'm fairly certain that he put Ben up to this. If that's the case though, the whole evening would have to be a setup, and I've been having such a good time that I don't want to believe it. Caleb shrugs innocently, like this is all a complete surprise to him. Stupidly, perhaps, I believe that it is.

"I'm a software developer," I tell him. Because I don't want him to get the idea that I'm looking for a job, I quickly add, "I freelance."

Ben's eyes light up, like he's a kid at Christmas. Unless he's a really good actor, no way was this a set up, and that realization makes me relax back against Caleb's arm, which is slung across the back of my chair.

"Do you have a lot of projects lined up?"

"I'm booked out until December," I lie. Well, it's not a complete lie; I do have a few projects that I'm working on, but I'm not completely booked out. I just don't want Ben to know that.

Ben nods. "I'm always looking for talent at my company," he says, as he reaches into his jacket and pulls out a card. "If you ever decide you want to try something other than the freelancing, give me a call. I'd love to take a look at your work."

I take the card, and get a look at the name. Ben *Williams*? Oh god, I'm a huge fan of his work. His firm has been involved in some truly cutting-edge development. It's all I can do not to squee, and tell him I'll drop everything for a chance to learn from him.

"Always selling something," Caleb says, shaking his head.

I slip the card into my purse, because maybe someday I'll be able to…

"Don't tell me you don't have a stack of cards in your jacket," Ben says accusingly, before taking a sip of wine. "If you say no, I'll know you're lying."

All Caleb says is, "I have more sense than to pull them out at dinner."

Ben rolls his eyes. "You're acting like I pulled out my-"

"Mia," Felicity says loudly, turning to me to distract the two of us from the testosterone that seems to be on overload tonight. "Why don't we go out for lunch soon? Maybe do a little shopping after?"

I smile at Felicity. In the background, Ben and Caleb are going on about something else now, thankfully. "I'd like that."

CHAPTER Thirteen

When we get back to Caleb's apartment, the first thing I see when we walk through the door is my bag safely resting in the corner of the foyer. Caleb jokingly put it there, teasing me about how it would be the first thing to welcome us back when we returned. And here it is. Safe.

"Feel better?" he asks, an amused lilt to his voice.

"I do."

Caleb slides his arm around my waist, pushes my hair over my shoulder, then starts kissing and sucking the back of my neck. My back is pressed against his chest, and I lean against him as his hand snakes across my ribs before it cups my breast. I gasp when his thumb slides across my nipple, all the while feeling Caleb smiling against me.

The cut of the dress that I'm wearing doesn't really allow for a bra, so I usually go without. Tonight is no exception, and

Caleb is taking full advantage of that, cupping and caressing me with only the thin fabric of my dress between his hand and my skin.

"I've been wanting you all night," he says. His voice is low, rumbly, and full of desire. It makes all the hairs on my body stand on end. "I've been waiting to have you all to myself again."

"You have me," I tell him, my voice a breathy whisper.

"Mmmm, I do. Now what am I going to do with you?" His breath is warm against my ear, making me shiver. "I love this dress so much. I could see your nipples through it all night. I've been wanting to do this," he says, giving my nipple a little pinch. I arch my back, wanting to feel more of his hand on my breast, and my ass pushes back against his erection, making him groan.

"Caleb?" I ask.

He's skimming his chin along the crook of my neck, teasing, scratching me with his stubble. "Yeah?"

"What else have you been wanting to do?"

"This," he says, sliding his deft hands down my sides, until they reach the hem of my dress. He pulls it up, until the fabric is bunched around my waist, then reaches for my underwear. "Fuck, Mia. You're not wearing any-"

"Surprise," I reply, feeling smug.

He cups my cheek, turning my head so he can reach my mouth and cover it with hot, lingering kisses. "I can't believe you went out like this."

"Why, are you jealous?" I'm really turned on, but I also wouldn't mind having a little argument right now. I think that could only stoke the fire building inside of me.

"I'm just glad I'm the lucky bastard you came home with."

Oh, an argument would be such a waste. These, *these* are the words I want to hear. "So lucky," I tell him.

He slips one arm around my waist, bringing my ass in contact with his erection again as his other hand finds its way between my legs. I let out a soft moan as Caleb's fingers work their magic on me.

"Fuck, you're wet already."

"I have been for a while," I say, reaching back and stroking his cock through his pants. I only manage three passes before he pulls away, and I hear the frantic unbuckling of his belt and unzipping of his zipper behind me.

Caleb growls, nipping my earlobe. "I want you. Now."

"Then have me," I tell him, hoping the low, raspy tone in my voice will spur him on. I turn my head and glance over my shoulder. My breath catches as I get a good look at Caleb, all hard and impatient as he rips open a condom and rolls it on.

"Face the wall," he says gruffly. "Brace yourself against it."

I'm already so turned on, but Caleb telling me what to do, well…that dials everything up about 10 more notches. I do what he says, letting my fingers spread out for leverage as I place my hands against the wall.

"Good." He slides his hand down my back, making my ass arch out toward him. He reaches down and runs his hands up the insides of my thighs. "Spread your legs."

Slowly, Caleb's arm finds its way across my middle, pulling me back, close to his body. He's so warm, and I just want his skin against mine, but it seems like he has other plans for now. I spread my legs for him, and the second I do, I'm rewarded with his lips pressing kisses along the crook of my neck.

"How do you want me to fuck you?" he asks.

My eyes flutter shut. I fight the urge to tell him to take me any way he wants, because I feel like I'll only drag this out if I'm anything less than incredibly specific. "Fast," I tell him. This isn't going to be about tender touches and teasing. This is about hot, insatiable need. "Hard."

Caleb slides the head of his cock along my slit, pressing it against my clit to the point where I'm pushing back into him, desperate for more.

"Please," I beg.

Just that one little word sets Caleb off, and he pushes into me, making us both groan.

"More," I gasp. "Harder."

That's all the encouragement he needs. He's holding onto me tightly, pounding his hips against me.

"You feel so good, Mia." He's practically breathless.

He feels amazing to me, stretching me, hitting me so deep in just the right spot.

"Make me feel *better*," I breathe.

Even in his frantic hurry to fuck me, he manages to exhale a little laugh, but he does exactly what I ask him to. He starts stroking my clit, his other hand gripping my breast. The fabric of my dress rubs against my nipples, making them harder. He keeps working my clit as he pounds into me, and it's all too much. I let my head fall back to rest against Caleb's shoulder, leaving my neck open for the taking, because it seems to be his favorite spot.

"I'm…I…"

"You gonna come?" he asks. His voice is thready and tight, like he's holding on by a string, staving off his orgasm until I have mine.

"Yeah. Yes, just…"

Like he knows what I'm going to ask him for, he rubs my clit a little harder, a little faster, and before I know it I'm falling apart in his arms. He lets me ride it out, and then I feel him stiffen behind me, his hips stuttering in an unfocused rhythm as he comes.

After, I'm leaning against the wall with my head pressed against it, my body too weak to hold itself up without assistance. Caleb turns me in his arms, and gives me a soft, breathless kiss.

"I was bored the day we met," he says, looking down at me with heavy-lidded eyes. "I walked into that bar on a whim."

I want to tell him that I'm glad he did, but I keep my mouth shut until he says what it is he wants to say.

"I don't have a history of making good decisions in bars," he admits, his nose brushing against mine before he leans in for another kiss. "But now I do."

CHAPTER *Fourteen*

"I wish you would let me come and pick you up," Caleb says. "I'm leaving the office now, I can come and get you on my way home."

"No, it's okay," I tell him. "It's out of the way, and will take longer. Besides, I'm already on my way to you." I've been staying in this shitty hotel for almost three weeks now, and all of my tracking programs are showing the same thing that they have since I left Chicago: absolutely nothing. Every day I feel braver, am a little less paranoid when I step out into public. I'm willing to leave some of my clothes in the hotel at this point, but never my computer. I still carry it everywhere with me, but every day I think that maybe, maybe someday soon I'll feel comfortable walking around without it. Every day I think maybe this will all turn out okay.

I blatantly ignore the fact that at some point I'm going to

have to deal with the friends I left back home, who are going to wonder what happened to me, and why I haven't come back. I wonder if I could gradually phase them out, and just lose touch with them. The thought of not going back home again gives me this pang of sadness in my belly, but it's better than the alternative. If not being able to go back to Chicago is the only price I wind up paying for what I did, then I'm going to consider myself truly lucky.

"Mia," Caleb says, sounding exasperated. He doesn't like me walking alone when he can send the car for me, I know this.

"You can keep me company while I walk." I'm hoping that agreeing to stay on the phone while I walk will placate him.

"Okay," he says warily. "Tell me about your day."

"I did some coding, ventured out into the sunlight to get a salad at the deli on the corner. I talked to a friend for a little while. That's pretty much it."

"Sounds exciting," he says dryly.

"The most exciting part of my day usually comes at night." I'm grinning, because the thought of going to see him makes me feel like wild butterflies have taken up residence in my stomach. It's like I don't have a care in the world.

"Literally," he replies.

"Literally," I repeat, laughing. "How was your day?"

"Too long. I sat through never-ending conference calls, and all I could think about was you."

"I'll be there soon enough," I tell him. "I just wanted to get some fresh air, and I'll be there in no time. What was your conference call about?"

"I don't want you to fall asleep while you're walking."

I laugh. "Please, tell me."

As he recounts the business of his day, I hustle, trying to make it a few more blocks, so my cab fare the rest of the way is cheaper. I like listening to the steady sound of Caleb's voice; I get lost in it, even, to the point where I'm just going through the motions of walking, not really paying much attention to what I'm doing. Vaguely, I hear the thrum of running footsteps, but I don't pay them any mind.

All of a sudden, there's a hard tug on my arm, and I feel the straps of my bag slide down. I manage to catch it with my hand, and tug. I know this is a stupid thing to do, and I know it goes against every single piece of advice about being robbed that I've ever heard, that no material thing is worth my life.

"No," I yell. "No!"

In the background, through the speaker of my phone, Caleb is frantically calling my name.

I can't see the face of the man who is robbing me; I only get a glimpse of his jaw as his fist connects with my face. I fall to the ground, my head hitting something hard, and then everything goes black.

CHAPTER *Fifteen*

My head feels stuffy and full, like every available bit of space inside of it is packed with cotton. The right side of my face is throbbing, and I know it's swollen, because the skin feels stretched to its limit. I think the entire right side of my face might explode at any moment. I manage to open my eyes just a sliver, hoping that I'll be able to figure out exactly where I am. Even the little bit of light that finds its way in is so bright that it actually hurts. There's a dull throb at the base of my neck, and everything combined has completely sapped whatever strength I had in me. I know that if I try to push myself any further right now that I'll wind up being in more pain than I already am.

Instead of focusing on everything that's wrong right now, I focus on the warm, steady weight on my right hand. All of my energy goes toward that warmth, and moving my fingers to hold onto it tightly. There are calluses beneath my fingertips, and I know without a doubt that I'm holding Caleb's hand. Or, he's holding mine. I suppose it doesn't matter. The thought of him sitting here with me—wherever it is that I am—brings me such comfort that all my panic completely subsides. He's here, and I'm safe. I *know* this. I'd like to smile at him, but I can't get the right muscles to move.

Instead, I close my eyes, sink back into the softness of the pillows behind my head, and I let myself drift.

I pass in and out of consciousness for a while, vaguely aware of what's going on around me. Sometimes I'm dragged out of sleep because I hear a strange voice, or loud beeping, or because soft hands are gently prodding at my wrist. Most of it's just background noise. Eventually, the room seems a bit dimmer than it was earlier, and I'm able to open my eyes without the blinding pain that accompanied the action earlier. I turn my head—or try to, at least—and let out a soft moan, because…ouch.

"Mia?"

The voice belongs to Caleb, and he's still clasping my hand. I feel his touch on my face, cupping my cheek as the pad of his thumb slides across my cheekbone. My eyelids flutter open, and yeah. That hurts. Too much light, just…too much everything.

I manage to make a sound that comes out kind of like,

"Mrphf."

When my vision clears, all I can see is Caleb's face, full of worry. "Shh," he says gently. "Don't try to talk. You're safe. You're going to be okay."

Going to be okay? My eyes widen, and he must read the surprise on my face, because...how did I get here in the first place?

"You hit your head, Mia," he says, sounding about as scared as I feel. "Someone pushed you, and you cracked your head against the cement. There isn't anything abnormal on any of your scans, but the doctor wants to keep you overnight. Do you remember what happened?"

I have to push through the drug-induced cobwebs that are clouding my mind, and think incredibly hard. It's like the memories are there, just out of reach. I can almost grab onto them, clasp them between my fingers as they threaten to float away. It takes everything I've got in me to focus on remembering whatever it was that landed me in here.

I remember walking, and talking to Caleb on the phone. I was going to his place, I think, or...meeting him for dinner. I feel like we might've argued about something...a car. I remember, he wanted to send a car to pick me up, but I wanted to walk...

Oh god.

Oh my god.

My bag. Someone ripped my bag off of my shoulder and

ran off with it, after punching me in the face and apparently leaving me unconscious on the sidewalk. My head is throbbing, seemingly in time with my racing heart, and when I sit up I think my brain might burst right out of my skull.

"My bag," I say, trying to swing my legs over the side of the bed, because that seems like something that might quell the nausea. All it manages to do is make me feel like I'm going to pass out.

"Mia," Caleb says soothingly, standing up so he can rub my back. That makes me feel marginally better, but not much. "Don't get worked up. We can replace your things."

I shake my head weakly, as much as the unrelenting throbbing will allow. "You don't understand," I tell him, unable to stop the tears that are streaming down my face.

Caleb looks confused, and desperate to help me. Desperate to make it better. "Whatever was in there, I can replace, Mia. I'll help you, please don't be upset. You're…you're going to make things worse."

I'm safe, I'm cared for, and apparently I'm going to get out of this with nothing more than a swollen face and a headache. I know things could be worse. I *know* they could, but desperation is closing in, making my chest tight, tugging at whatever rational thought is left inside of me.

"It was everything I had," I say quietly, telling Caleb more than I know I should. I think the painkillers combined with the head trauma are making it difficult for me to keep my damn mouth shut. "You don't understand."

Caleb opens his mouth to reply, but a nurse walks in, effectively cutting him off. She's a friendly, older woman with short white hair. "What's the matter?" she asks. The kindness on her face and in her voice immediately puts me at ease. "You've gotten yourself all worked up, and that's not good. Take deep breaths," she says as she inhales, and motions to her chest, indicating that I should follow her lead.

I do exactly as she does. Deep inhale, deep exhale. Over and over again.

"Let's see if we can get something to calm you down, okay?"

I nod. Being calm sounds really good right now, and I definitely need pharmaceutical help to get me there. "Okay."

When the nurse leaves the room, Caleb helps me lie back on the bed, and smooths my hair off of my face.

I lean into his touch. "What's wrong with me?"

"They want to make sure your head is okay," he says quietly. He's very patient, despite the fact that I get the feeling I've asked him that before, and he had already given me an answer. "You also have some swelling around your cheekbone and your eye."

"I can tell," I say as I reach up to feel for the damage, but Caleb catches my hand and folds his fingers through mine. "How did you find me?"

"I was on the phone with you, when…" he trails off. I

realize for the first time since I woke up that he must've heard everything that happened to me while he was on the phone. "A nice woman stayed on the phone with me to let me know what was happening after she called nine-one-one. I arrived at the hospital right as they were bringing you in."

"Oh," I reply, feeling like I'm on the verge of tears. My emotions are all over the place, and they feel absolutely unstoppable.

"It's going to be okay."

Caleb is really good at this whole soothing me in crisis thing. I decide that he's the person that I want to have around for any other kind of emergency I might have in my life. Emergency. Shit - I just remembered that my insurance card was in my bag, along with my ID.

"My wallet's gone, too. I don't know my insurance information," I say, hysteria creeping back into my voice.

"I took care of everything, you don't have to worry about it."

I'm going to have to figure out how much all of this is costing and pay him back. I'm determined to do that once I get my life in order, no matter how long it takes.

"Is there anyone you want me to call?" he asks. "Your parents? A friend?"

The soft, gentle way he's talking to me makes me want to drift off to sleep again. It's so relaxing that I think I might not even need whatever medication the nurse has gone to get for me.

"My parents are dead," I tell him, unable to stop myself. I definitely don't want him calling Marcus. "So there's no one." It hurts to realize exactly how true that is. "Will you stay with me?"

He grips my hand tightly, and says, "Of course I will."

CHAPTER Sixteen

I'm sitting on the edge of my bed, fully dressed in the clothes I had been wearing the night I was robbed. Caleb had been kind enough to have them cleaned, but wearing them still feels wrong. I'm being discharged today, after two days of observation. My brain activity is fine, and the swelling on my face is going down. I'm getting better, despite the fact that the bruises on my cheek and eye are blooming an angry, deep purple.

I feel oddly detached from everything at the moment. Caleb is standing across from me, listening intently to the nurse as she describes my care instructions to him. It's funny that I've spent the past month or so on the run from an actual hitman, but a common street criminal was able to bring me down first. Luckily I had a stash of cash and a credit card in my pocket, and I still have my burner phone that I can contact

Marcus on, but my computer…god, my computer is gone.

Thankfully, the hard drive will overwrite itself if anyone other than me tries to sign in on it, and I do have backups of all my programs stored safely in the cloud. There's just the small issue of not having enough cash to replace the machine that I had. I could charge the parts, sure, but do I risk putting a transaction with my name on it out there for Privya to find? I could take a train to Connecticut or something, and take out a cash advance there. But then I'd risk him knowing where in the country I am, and…maybe he doesn't know. Maybe I'm worrying for nothing.

"Miss Briggs?" I hear the nurse say.

I shake head, pulling myself out of my thoughts. The nurse is looking at me patiently, with a faint smile. Caleb is looking at me like he's not sure I should be allowed to leave this hospital.

"Yes?" I say, distractedly.

"You need to come back immediately if you experience any of the symptoms on this sheet," the nurse replies, pointing to a piece of paper that Caleb is holding in his hands. "Understood?"

I nod.

"You're going to be staying with Mister Simmons?" she asks, nodding at Caleb.

"She is." Caleb gives me a look that's nearly a glare, just daring me to say otherwise. He insisted on me staying with him while I recuperated, and I fought him on it. It's too soon, it's too much, but at the same time…where else am I going to go? I'm low on funds, and my prospects are looking pretty bleak right now. It was a superficial fight. I want to stay with him, and, as much as I hate it, I need to stay with him.

"All right," the nurse says, as an orderly shows up with a wheelchair.

"Is this really necessary?" I ask.

Caleb gives me that look again, the one that's just daring me to put up a fight. The nurse quickly tells me that it's hospital policy, and that if I want to get out of this place, I'm going to have to do it in a wheelchair.

If it's my only means of escaping? I'll happily let someone take me for a ride.

"You're going to have your hands full with this one," the nurse tells Caleb.

Caleb looks at me fondly, like there isn't anything in the world that he would change about me, and it makes a warm rush of some unnamed emotion flow through me. He walks ahead to get an elevator for us, and as she pushes me through the door and down the hallway, the nurse leans down and whispers in my ear. "You've got a good one here, honey. You better hold onto him."

I know Caleb is going to have some questions for me that I'm not going to want to answer. I wonder how long I'll be hanging on to him after that.

Caleb and I are quiet on our way back to his apartment, but he holds my hand in the back of the town car as we ride along the busy streets of Manhattan. When we arrive at his building, I follow him inside. It feels strange being here like this, since I'm not here for a visit, I'm here to stay for however long I need or want to, or until I wear out my welcome. I feel naked without my bag, and for as much as Caleb used to tease me about it, he hasn't breathed a word of it since the short conversation we had after I woke up in the hospital room, where I told him that it was all that I had. Maybe he thinks I don't remember telling him that, but either way, I'm grateful to not have to answer questions about that statement right now.

It's kind of like a raincloud hanging over my head. I know it's going to start pouring at some point, but I'm hoping to stay dry for as long as I can.

I step inside Caleb's apartment, feeling uncomfortable with my empty handedness. I'm here for an extended stay, but I don't have anything with me. I didn't have anything to bring with me, except for the clothes I left at my hotel. I never did check out of there, and only paid by the night, so I'm guessing the clothes I did have with me have been tossed or donated. Yet another strike against me.

When the door closes behind us, Caleb makes a show of locking it. It's a touching gesture; even though we're in a secured building on a floor high in the sky, he still wants me to feel safe here.

Caleb steps up to me, and pulls me into his arms.

"You're safe here," he says. He's holding me as tightly as he dares, and apart from handholding while I was bedridden, it's the most prolonged contact we've had in days.

"I know," I reply with a grateful sigh. "Thank you for letting me stay here. I'm not quite ready to go back to the hotel."

I feel his muscles stiffen as soon as the words leave my mouth, so I know I've said something wrong, but I don't know what.

"You're not going back to the hotel," he says firmly. There's a hard, unwavering glint in his eyes, like he's just daring me to challenge him on this.

I take a deep breath to get a grip on my rapidly fraying nerves. I might be scared and borderline desperate, but, "You don't get to tell me what to do, Caleb."

I'm not sure whether I step out of his arms or he steps out of mine, but before I know it, we're standing with a few inches (that feel like a mile) between us.

"Excuse me?"

"You heard me!" I yell. I feel like I'm on some kind of emotional roller coaster, and I can't tell which end is up. I'm angry, and I can't get a handle on that, but why am I upset? Caleb cares about me, he just wants me to be safe, but this sets a bad precedent. He can't just command me to do things his way just because he's scared and worried. "If I want to go back to the hotel, I'll go back to the hotel. You don't get to tell me what to do now, especially not if that's going to be a requirement for your hospitality."

His eyes widen. "You think I want to control you?"

"Isn't that what you're doing? Is there some other way that I'm supposed to interpret you telling me that I can't go back to my hotel if I want to?"

"Please," he says, gritting his teeth. "Don't fight me on this."

Those are the exact words that make me *want* to fight him on this. I'm feeling the last bit of my control slipping through my fingertips, and all I need is just a minute of quiet to collect my thoughts and work through them, but Caleb isn't going to give that to me. I walk toward the door, not really sure where I'll go once I step outside of it, but needing to move, to-

"Mia," Caleb says, and the desperation in his voice is enough to get me to stop. "I'm your boyfriend, I'm not about to let you go out to a strange hotel right after you've been robbed when I have a nice and safe place for you to stay right here!"

I can't feel or hear anything apart from the rush of blood in my ears. He's my *boyfriend*? We've never even discussed anything like that, even though I obviously haven't been seeing anyone else, and given the amount of time he spends with me, Caleb can't be, either. We've known each other for almost a month, but I still haven't come clean with him about the real reason why I'm here. I'm not sure how much longer I can keep it from him, and I feel terrible taking him up on his kindness when I haven't even been honest with him. Hearing him call himself my boyfriend knowing all that seems like too much, and yet it makes a flood of warmth flow through my veins.

I like the word, like hearing him talking about belonging to me.

"You're my boyfriend now?" I ask. My voice sounds accusatory and mean in a way that I wasn't intending.

Caleb looks like I've actually hit him. "Aren't I?"

"We never talked about it, I just-"

"I assumed." He takes a long, deep breath, like he's trying to calm himself down. "Is that not where this is headed for you?"

"No, it's not that. I just didn't know that was where this was headed for *you*."

Caleb's eyebrows scrunch together. "Have I somehow been unclear about my intentions? You're the only woman in my life. You're the only woman I want to *be* in my life."

My heart is hammering in my chest, and I feel like I might pass out. I had figured we were on our way to getting serious, but I had been avoiding thinking about that, because I didn't want to deal with the fact that this thing that Caleb and I are building together is standing on a foundation full of cracks. Cracks that I put there by not being honest with him about why I'm here in the city, why I ran away from Chicago. What am I going to do? Stay and let my shadowy past lurk out there in the distance somewhere, wondering if I've run so far that it can't ever catch up with me? Tell him I'm a thief and lose him forever?

"You haven't been unclear about your intentions," I say,

looking down at my hands.

"Do you not want the same things I want?"

Those clear green eyes of his are boring into mine, and all I want to do is give him an answer, but answers come with consequences that I'm not ready to deal with yet. "I want you," I tell him.

He takes a deep breath. "Only me?"

I give him a grin, then reach out and twine our fingers together. "Only you."

Caleb leans down and gives me a sweet, tender kiss. "Please stay. It's not that I'm trying to control you, Mia. This is for me. Please do this for me."

"Caleb, I-"

"Don't make me listen to someone hurting you over the phone again. Please."

When I see the genuine pain in his eyes, I'm nearly left breathless. Of course hearing what happened to me over the phone scared him. Even though things are still incredibly new between us, I wouldn't want to listen to him getting robbed and beaten while I was on the other end of the line, helpless. Just the thought of it makes my stomach roll.

"Okay," I tell him, and he looks absolutely relieved.

"Come here," he says softly. He guides me through the apartment, down the hallway that leads to his bedroom. There's a room on the left, near the middle of the hallway, and the door has been closed every time I've been here.

Today, he opens it. Inside is a spare bedroom. It's a beautiful space; sunlight floods the room. Everything is neutral, from the hardwood floors, to the beige walls, to the off-white comforter that covers the bed. The large, wrought-iron headboard is the focal point of the room, and it is framed by two large, floor-to-ceiling windows. There's a vase full of daisies on the nightstand to the right of the bed, and I grin, because I made an offhanded comment not too long ago that they're my favorite. But…why are they in here?

"What's this?"

Caleb looks at me with a bashful smile. "It's your room."

My eyes widen, and my stomach drops. I figured that when he asked me to stay, he was asking me to stay with *him*. As in sleep with him, sleep in his room and in his bed, like I have been.

"*My room*," I repeat dumbly. "Do you not want…" I'm having difficulty forming the words for the rest of that question. Did we not just decide that he's officially my boyfriend?

Caleb shrugs. "You seemed to want to stay in your hotel a lot, and I figured it was because you wanted some time away from me. I thought it would be good for you to have a place to escape to, if you wanted."

"Oh," I sigh. "Caleb, that's not why."

I wait for him to ask me why I spent so much time in my own hotel room when I could've been spending time with him, but he doesn't. He just says, "I want you in my bed, Mia."

The words send a wave of desire through me, even though my face is swollen and the color of an eggplant, and I know for sure sex is off the table for the foreseeable future. But when a handsome, kind man says something like that, how can I not go weak in the knees?

"I want to be in your bed."

"Good," he replies, leaning down and placing a quick kiss on my lips. "But if you need some time to yourself, this room is all yours."

Right now it feels like time to myself is the very last thing I need.

CHAPTER Seventeen

When I wake up, I hear voices echoing all the way down the hall into the bedroom. The door is open, and I figure Caleb left it like that so he could hear me if I called for him. The fact that he's so thoughtful makes me smile, despite the crankiness I usually feel when I first wake up. Last night was my first night as a temporary resident in Caleb's apartment, and he told me that he was going to be working from home for the next few days in order to keep an eye on me. So, I'm not exactly surprised to hear his voice; I figured he would take a conference call or two during the day. What does surprise me is that there's someone responding to him when he speaks, and that someone is here in the apartment.

I glance back at the clock, surprised to see that I've slept so late into the morning. I've always been an early riser, but Caleb's thick, lined curtains keep the sun from shining through and waking me up like it normally does.

Slowly, I begin the process of getting out of bed. The nurse was adamant that I not move too quickly for the first few days I'm home. I move my legs across the soft sheets, until they dangle off the side of the bed. When I'm feeling confident that I'm not going to be dizzy or pass out when I step onto the floor, I slide down off of the mattress.

I'm only marginally woozy. The doctor said it's common and that it would pass soon enough. Honestly, I can't wait for that day to come.

The only clothes I have with me are the ones I was wearing when I was robbed, so I'm wearing a t-shirt that belongs to Caleb, and actually looks like an overly large dress on me.

Standing in the middle of the room, I notice that I can't hear the voices as clearly as I did before. Caleb is still talking to his guest, but I can only make out faint sounds of the conversation. Even though I know it's terrible to eavesdrop, I really can't help my curiosity, so I step out into the hallway and quietly walk toward the main living area.

The closer I get to the end of the hallway, the clearer those hushed voices are. When I'm at a place where I can get a good listen, I immediately recognize one of the voices as Ben's. The fact that they're being hush-hush about whatever it is that they're talking about makes me think that whatever it is that they're talking about is *me*.

When I get to the point where I can't walk any further

without the risk of being seen, I stop.

"What makes you think that?" Ben asks.

There's a long silence from Caleb, before he finally says, "She was just…carrying that bag around with her everywhere."

God, they *are* talking about me. And about my suspicious behavior with my bag, which…well, it can't be good.

"I can't blame her for not wanting to leave it at a hotel. My laptop is my livelihood too, and there isn't a chance in hell that I'd leave it where anyone who had access to my room could take it."

"I'm sure that drives Oliver crazy," he replies with an amused lilt in his voice.

"I've told him about it several times. He's always got some kind of rebuttal about how he screens his employees, and has top-of-the-line room safes, but I take an extreme stance on the safety of my electronics: trust no one."

"Still," Caleb continues. "She carried that bag around like it was the only thing she owned."

"What would be wrong with that?" Ben asks.

I barely even know the guy, and I feel like I have an ally. He could just be riling Caleb up by coming up with counterpoints to all of his concerns, but even the illusion that someone's in my corner feels nice. I like Ben more than I already did.

"I don't know," Caleb replies. "Don't you think she'd have some furniture stored somewhere? Or have movers bringing it here from Chicago? Something?"

"Have you ever asked if she has furniture stored somewhere? Or if movers are bringing it here from Chicago?"

This conversation is making me uneasy. Of course, I have given Caleb reason to be at least a little suspicious of me, what with the staying in hotels and carrying that damned bag everywhere. I had foolishly hoped that he wouldn't ever raise those suspicions. The good thing is that he doesn't sound angry about it; he's just trying to talk it out with his friend. I suppose I should be thankful for that; at least now I won't be blindsided if any of this ever comes up in conversation.

"I'm really trying not to push her too hard."

"I get it," Ben replies. "Maybe there are some things you should push, though."

Now I feel even worse than I already did about not being totally honest with him. He's offered me a place to stay despite his misgivings, and…god, I'm just so lucky to have met him. I'd be lucky anyway, but with the situation I'm in? It's the biggest blessing imaginable.

"Speaking of pushing, you really should talk her into letting me see some of her work. I've got this new project that I'm starting, and I'm short-handed. I need someone who knows what they're doing and can jump into the deep end right away."

"Yeah," Caleb says distractedly. "I'll see what I can do."

I've listened to too much, and overstepped my bounds enough for one day. I sneak down the hallway, and back into the bedroom, where I strip off Caleb's shirt and head straight into the bathroom. I need some time to think, and standing under the steady spray of a shower head always seems to do the trick. Once the water is steaming hot, just the way I like it, I step inside the shower.

As I wash the hospital off, I try to figure out what exactly I'm going to do when Caleb starts asking questions.

It seems like I'm running out of time.

My eyes are glued to the top-of-the-line, custom-built laptop that Caleb just placed in front of me on the dining room table. It's the nicest one I've ever had; even nicer than the one I built myself with special-ordered parts that I spent *months* saving up for. This thing runs like a dream. I'm half expecting a ray of light to shine down on it from heaven, complete with a choir of angels singing in the background. That's how amazing this laptop is.

"How did you get this?" I ask. The person that built this beauty has some serious computer know-how. It's not exactly surprising that Caleb would have access to something like this, but to get it on such short notice is impressive.

Caleb grins at me, and shrugs. "I asked Ben if he could put something together for you. I knew you'd need a new one after…after."

It hasn't escaped my notice that Caleb has trouble actually

voicing what happened to me. He seems to do just fine until he gets to the part where he needs to utter the word "robbed." Maybe it's not necessarily an issue for him; maybe he's worried that saying the word is going to cause me some kind of undue stress. I have to admit that even now, days later, when the swelling is going down and the bruises are fading, I can admit that it's a little amusing that for as much as I worried about Privya tracking me down here, I got hurt by a common street criminal.

"I can't accept this, Caleb," I tell him. There isn't any conviction behind my refusal, because I don't really mean it. This machine is beautiful, and I need it almost as much as I need air. Apart from wanting to keep my tracking programs running, I do have actual work to finish for a few clients. I need the income, but Caleb has already been far too generous with me. He's taking care of my hospital tab, he's given me a place to stay…this seems like too much.

"The way you're looking at it says otherwise," he replies, and I can hear his pleased grin in his voice.

Caleb is right. I'm weak. I'm going to accept it, and use the hell out of it. He's gone to such great lengths to make sure I feel comfortable and safe since I've been here, it would be rude to refuse this gift, extravagant as it may be.

"Thank you." I lean over and press a tender kiss against his lips. "You're very thoughtful, and this is absolutely perfect. It's what I would've made for myself if I could have-" I stop that sentence right in its tracks, because I don't want the 'afforded it' to come off like some kind of backhanded swipe against his wealth and generosity. "And thank Ben for me, please. I mean, I'll thank him myself the next time I see him, but in case that's not for a while, or if I don't-"

"You're going to see him again."

I nod. Even though Caleb is grinning at me, there's something clouding his features, some kind of conflict that he's not voicing. It probably has something to do with the conversation that I eavesdropped on earlier this morning between him and Ben. I want to ask what's troubling him, but I'm worried that I'll accidentally wind up revealing that I was listening to them while Caleb thought I was sleeping. If he has something to ask me, he'll ask in his own time.

"I'm going to leave you to it," Caleb says as he stands up. He leans over and presses a kiss to the top of my head. "Get yourself all situated here; you look like a kid on Christmas."

I give his hand a squeeze as he walks away, then immediately give the full weight of my attention to my new baby. The computer is already hooked up to Caleb's wifi, so I log into my secured cloud account and queue my programs for download in the order of their priority. I'm just about to see what this thing can really do, when Caleb leans against the doorway.

"Mia?"

"Yeah?"

He swallows so hard that I can actually see his Adam's apple bobbing. "You'd tell me if you were in trouble, wouldn't you?"

"What?" I ask, pretending to be perplexed by the question, in order to give myself more time to answer it.

"If you were in trouble, you'd tell me, wouldn't you?"

Oh, here goes. "What makes you think that I'm in trouble?"

Taking a deep breath, he steps back into the room, and stands across from me, on the other side of the table. All the good feelings I had just a few moments earlier disappear, because I can tell I'm about to be called out on something. Oddly enough, I don't panic. I want to be as honest with him as I can without dragging him into the mess I've made for myself.

"Why did you lie to me about which hotel you were staying in?"

I'm instantly relieved, because he's not asking me if I'm in *trouble* trouble, he's asking me if I'm in financial trouble, given the fact that he knows that I traded in staying at Oliver's 5-star hotel for the shit hole that I moved into after. Assuming he figured out which hotel that was, which…maybe he didn't.

Either way, I can at least be honest about this, no matter how difficult it is.

"How did you know about that?"

All the visible tension in his shoulders immediately melts away, and he moves closer, taking the same seat that he had just vacated. I turn and face him, and he cradles my hands in his, his eyes all open and full of kindness.

"When you were in the hospital, I called them to check you out, because I didn't see much point in you paying for a room you weren't staying in. I asked if I could come and pick up any clothes that you had left behind, and they told me that no one with your name was staying there."

I suppose it says a lot about his level of trust in me that he didn't ask me if the reason the hotel clerk couldn't find my reservation is because I was checked in under an alias. I was checked in under an alias, but not at the hotel he thinks I was staying at, so I suppose that doesn't matter.

There's a lump in my throat. Even though he's being so kind to me, I can't help feeling embarrassed about this admission. "I had to check out of the hotel I was staying at when we met. I couldn't afford to keep staying there, and every hotel in the city is so expensive. I…I was kind of ashamed to tell you that I was staying in a not-so-nice place because of financial reasons."

"You don't have to be embarrassed," he says gently. "If I had known, I would've helped you."

"I didn't want that," I say. "I don't want that."

"I just…" I don't want to be a charity case. I don't want things to be even more unequal between us. I have a slew of reasons for feeling this way, but I can't seem to voice any of them at the moment.

"I assumed you had an apartment lined up and were living in a hotel until it was ready for you to move in. I'm not sure why I assumed that; I should've asked."

Shrugging, I look down at our hands. "I came here on a whim. I didn't have housing of any kind lined up."

"What?" he asks, almost amused, like he can't believe I'd just uproot my life like that. I wouldn't have, if I had any choice.

"I needed to get away, and come someplace new," I explain, hoping he'll understand. "I wasn't sure how long I was going to stay."

"Oh," he replies. He's clearly shellshocked - that wasn't the response he was expecting to hear from me.

"You make me want to stay."

"Why didn't you tell me?"

I press my lips together as I figure out how I'm going to explain this to him. "How would that have looked to you? You have all this." I wave my hand at his...*everything.* "I didn't want you to think I was taking advantage of your kindness. I would never take advantage of you like that."

"Asking for help isn't taking advantage, Mia," he says. "Trust me, people have taken advantage of me a lot in my lifetime. I know what it looks like. And I've had to lean on people, too. I would never judge you for that."

"You don't even know me." I look up at him with watery eyes, because...how is this man even real? "We were practically strangers."

Caleb crooks his fingers under my chin, and tilts my head up, but I refuse to meet his eyes. "Hey. Mia." He waits patiently for me to look at him, and when I finally do, he says, "We're not strangers anymore. I don't do the things we've done with strangers."

I reluctantly smile, and okay. He wins. "I don't either."

Caleb is smiling too, and all the heaviness that was in the air a few moments ago dissipates. "Since we're not strangers, and we established yesterday that I am, in fact, your boyfriend, I'd like you to do something for me."

"Anything."

"Felicity called to check up on you and see how you're doing."

"That was nice of her," I reply. "But that doesn't sound at all like a favor."

Caleb lets out a short breath of a laugh. "She wanted me to ask you if you'd feel up to getting out of the house tomorrow."

"O…kay." I'm confused about where this is going, but it would be nice to get some fresh air and take a walk.

"Since I know you have a limited wardrobe right now, I asked her if she wanted to go shopping with you. She's a pro. Literally. She's been doing my shopping for years, and she's had my credit card numbers memorized for even longer than that," he explains with a fond look on his face. He must really care about her.

"Caleb-"

"I know you're going to tell me you can't, but you *can*," he says softly. "All you have to do is say yes."

I'm still not convinced. I do need clothes, but…

"It's not a completely selfless proposition," he admits. "I'm going to need you to find a replacement for that dress of yours I liked so much."

That makes me smile.

Sensing a weakness like the businessman that he is, he asks, "Is that a yes?"

"Yes."

"No," I say adamantly. I feel like this is an incredibly polite response since what I really want to say is *hell no*.

Caleb just crosses his arms over his chest and gives me a look that I'm sure has made countless strong-willed businessmen cower in the shadows of their corner offices. That look won't work on me. Not when it comes to this. "It's non-negotiable."

"I said *no*, Caleb. Remember that conversation we had just the other day about how you don't get to control me?"

"Mia," he replies imploringly. He takes a step forward, and takes my hands in his. "Remember the other part of that conversation, where I asked you not to make me listen on the other end of the line while somebody robbed and beat you?"

Damn it. "You can't keep using that argument whenever

you're not getting your way."

"I'll only use it when it comes to keeping you safe, which is all I'm trying to do."

I take a deep breath, and give the man who Caleb hired to be my bodyguard for the day a once over. My dad would say that he's built like a brick shit house, and there isn't any doubt in my mind that he'd be able to keep me from harm. He kind of looks like he could stop a bullet without much effort or injury. Nevertheless, I don't want him following me and Felicity around all day, no matter how huge or handsome or friendly looking he is.

"People get robbed here every day," I tell Caleb. "They weren't after me, they were just after my things." I'm fully aware that might not always be the case, though. Someday soon—today, even—someone could be after *me*, but when that happens, I don't want Caleb or some security person he's hired to be dragged into it. "The chances of it happening again are slim."

Caleb kisses me on the forehead. "I'm not taking any chances, no matter how slim they are. You won't even know he's there. Right, Stone?"

I look over at the man who is most likely going to be a close friend for the next few hours.

"Your name is Stone?" It's very soap opera, and it reminds me that I'm now living in some kind of surreal reality where I have a boyfriend who hires men named Stone to come shopping with me and keep me safe. It's absurd and adorable at the same time.

"It's my last name, ma'am."

"I'll make a deal with you," I say, as my gaze swings from Caleb to Stone. "I'll let you follow me around all day, as long as you call me by my first name, and I'll call you by yours."

Caleb sighs exasperatedly behind me, and the sound of it makes me want to smile. "That's not how this works, Mia."

"It's how this is going to work if you want me to agree."

Caleb gives Stone a curt nod.

"What's your first name, Stone?"

He looks so amused, I get the feeling that he spends his days with people who are perfectly willing to keep a wall of professionalism between themselves and him. I am not that person.

"It's Sam, ma'am."

"Sam," I say, delighted, as I reach out to shake his hand. "I'm Mia."

"Mia…" Caleb says testily.

"I know, I know. This isn't how it works." I narrow my eyes at him. "This is how it's working now." He nods and gives me a reluctant smile.

Sam shakes my hand. "It's a pleasure to meet you, ma'am."

"Mia." I'm going to get him to call me by my first name if it's the last thing I do.

"Yes, ma'am."

I sigh, and Caleb is grinning like he's won something. He leans in and kisses me, then straightens his tie.

"I'm going to the office for a bit. You have fun with Felicity. I'll see you later." He claps Sam on the shoulder as he passes him. "Best of luck, Stone. You're gonna need it."

"I'm not that bad," I tell him.

He smiles. "Well see about that…Mia."

I clap my hands together and somehow manage to squeal, which is more than a little embarrassing. Doesn't matter though; this feels like a victory.

Felicity and I spend the morning—and the better part of the afternoon—flitting between shops, filling up the trunk of Caleb's SUV with countless bags from trendy boutiques that Felicity insists we visit. I thought Caleb was being facetious when he said that she was a professional shopper, but when he said literally, he meant *literally*. She knows all the salespeople in all the stores we enter, and they even take us back to look through new arrivals that aren't out on the floor yet.

After she asks me how I'm feeling, I tell her I'm better. Getting better by the hour. So, she goes out of her way not to mention the robbery or my subsequent hospitalization, and successfully manages to avoid staring at the bruises on the side of my face that I wasn't able to fully cover with makeup this morning.

Sam stays in the periphery, just like Caleb promised he would be, and he almost cracks a smile when Felicity and I stop for ice cream and offer him a cup full of mint chip. It doesn't take long for the all-business scowl to come back though, just daring anyone to even look in our direction.

After we finish our ice cream, we move on to the last boutique of the day, one that Felicity's been talking about all afternoon.

"Caleb told me he was sending out the big guns, and I see that he meant it," she says, nodding in Sam's direction.

"The literal big guns," I reply as I flex my pathetic bicep and point at it. "He could probably crush someone with those muscles."

Felicity laughs. "Don't let Caleb hear you say that. He'll get jealous."

He probably would, and I don't plan on testing that theory to find out if we're right. "Caleb's got nothing to be jealous about. He's...perfect," I say. Even I can hear the dreaminess in my voice, so I'm not exactly surprised that Felicity picks up on it.

"Oh, you've got it bad," she teases. "It's good, though. That's good for Caleb. It's exactly what he needs." She's standing in front of a dress display, examining the cut of the fabric, and the way it hangs. I wonder if she's going to ask someone to model it for us. When she did that earlier, the store owner gave us champagne to sip as we watched a mini fashion show.

I wouldn't say no to something like that again.

"What do you mean that's exactly what he needs?"

She shrugs as she moves to examine the dress hanging next to the one she has apparently decided that she doesn't like. "He's always been a tough nut to crack, ever since he came to live with us after his parents' accident."

I know it's not possible, but I'm sure I feel my heart stop beating right in my chest. The air gets thick and difficult to breathe. I hadn't ever heard anything about an accident, and I'm not sure whether I should admit to that, or go along with what Felicity's saying like I know what she's talking about. No, I need to tell her that I wasn't aware of that, because if Caleb wanted me to know, he would've told me. After everything he's done for me since I met him, at the very least I owe him his privacy.

I must have some kind of shocked look on my face, something that makes it clear that I wasn't aware of whatever happened to Caleb's parents, because Felicity stops examining the dress in front of her, and freezes. She looks over at me, her mouth dropping into an O shape.

"You didn't know," she manages to say. "I'm sorry. I shouldn't have said anything, I just assumed he had already told you about all that."

"No, not yet." I move forward, and run my hand along the fabric of a gorgeous silk wrap dress, hoping to make the whole situation a little less awkward.

"What a terrible thing for me to let slip," she replies, looking absolutely stricken. With some other people, I might suspect a hidden agenda was at play, but Felicity looks genuinely upset that she said anything at all.

"It's okay, I won't say anything. If he wanted me to know, he would've said something. Clearly he's not there yet."

"You should definitely hear it from him instead of a bigmouth like me, I'm sorry. It wasn't my place to bring it up if he hasn't done it already."

I put my hand on her forearm and give her an understanding smile. "It's okay, honestly. I won't say anything, and I'll let him tell me in his own time. Don't feel bad; you're not used to censoring yourself about him, and things between Caleb and me are still kind of new. We've just been enjoying each other, and haven't really gotten to the part where we tell each other our deepest and darkest secrets yet."

I am the last person to judge Caleb for the things he hasn't told me, considering I have a laundry list of things I need to confess to him at some point, and I guarantee that my list? It's worse than his. All of this makes me realize that as far as we've come over the past month of knowing each other, we've still got a long way to go.

"I'm glad that he has someone who will keep his secrets," I tell Felicity, playfully bumping her shoulder to help lighten the mood. "It must be difficult to find that kind of loyalty living the life that he does."

"He's like my brother, but marginally less of a pain in the ass than Ben is," she says, laughing.

"Ben seems like a good guy." There aren't many people who would race to make the kind of machine he made for me on a few days' notice.

"He is," Felicity says, moving on to the next dress. She looks at the fabric thoughtfully, biting her lip in deep concentration. "It's funny, Ben had a tendency to be a little…let's call it *fickle*, when it came to his personal relationships. Caleb, he had a history of keeping people at arm's length. I'm glad he decided to be different with you."

With everything that's still unknown between Caleb and me, it's nice to know that my presence in his life has made a noticeable difference to the people who know and love him.

"I'm glad he decided to be different with me, too," I reply with a smile.

Felicity's phone buzzes. She pulls it out of her purse, and starts typing furiously. "I'm sorry, I know this is rude, but I've got an assignment due on Friday, and my partners and I have been trying to schedule time to get together to work on it."

I'm sure my mouth drops open in surprise, because I assumed she was out of college already, even though I hadn't ever asked.

"Don't look so surprised," she says, grinning.

"I…you just seem so…together. Not that college students aren't together—I didn't mean that at all—but you have your own business and all of these connections. I wouldn't have ever thought you were still in school."

Felicity laughs as she puts her phone back in her pocket. "I understand. Doing what I do requires a good eye and some taste, but you don't need a degree for it. My career choice has been a bone of contention between my father and me, and I'm getting my degree to prove that I'm serious. I'm learning more about the business side of things so I can expand and grow. I'm going to be a brand someday."

I grin at her. "Good for you. I think you'll be amazing at it, if today is any indication."

"It's such a spoiled little rich girl thing, you know? A personal shopper? Getting *paid* to buy things? I mean, it even makes *me* want to roll my eyes. I'm pretty sure I'll never hear the end of it from my family, but I don't want to be a joke. Not with them, not with anyone."

"I don't think anything about this is a joke," I tell her.

"You know that old adage, 'do what you love, and you'll never work a day in your life?'?"

I nod. That's why I got into software development. I love it, and it doesn't ever feel like work. Earning a living doing what you love is the greatest gift a person can give themselves. I know not everyone is lucky enough to be able to do that, but I'm glad that Felicity is able to.

"I love doing this. I have a knack for it, and people want to work with me. Styling people, searching for the right outfit for an occasion, I don't know...I know it's frivolous, but it makes me want...*more*."

"It's not frivolous to the people who hire you," I tell her.

"Yeah," she replies with a smile. "That's true. My dad thinks that sitting at a desk and cultivating a family legacy is the only way a person's professional life has any worth. But I'm going to cultivate my own legacy."

"I have no doubt that you will."

Felicity sighs, like some great burden is off her chest, and I get the feeling that she doesn't have very many people to talk to. I'm glad I could be that person today.

"Enough about me," she says, as she reaches forward and pulls a black gown off of its rack. "What do you think about this?"

The dress is almost too beautiful to touch, but I do it anyway. It's sleek with a flowing skirt, and a halter top with a neckline that scoops low enough to be revealing without revealing too much. The back is almost nonexistent, but still somehow manages to be tasteful. It's a dress that I wouldn't have picked out for myself in a million years, but it's gorgeous. I haven't even tried it on yet, and I want it.

"I think it's beautiful," I admit. "But I don't have any occasion to wear it." This is a special event dress, not something you throw on to go out to dinner.

"Well, you'll be happy to know that Caleb specifically requested that I pick out something just like this for you." She puts her hand on my shoulder, holds out the dress, and leads me toward the dressing area.

"What for?" I ask.

Felicity shrugs. "No idea, but we're shopping on his dime, so I do what I'm asked. Today I'm just a consultant, and the hired help, so if he wants me to buy a dress, we're buying a dress."

Far be it from me to turn down an offer like that.

CHAPTER *Nineteen*

"Looks like you had fun today," Caleb says, with an amused glint in his eyes as they roam over the piles of bags that Sam brought up from the car.

I feel self-conscious and embarrassed all of a sudden, and I can't really put my finger on why. Maybe it has something to do with the fact that I'm just now getting a good look at everything I brought home with me, and Caleb's the one who footed the bill. Maybe this wasn't what he was expecting? I think it's too much, but Felicity had insisted. Maybe Caleb thinks it's too much, too?

"I did have fun, although I think Felicity went a *little* overboard."

Caleb leans in, and kisses me softly. "I asked her to spoil you, so I think she's still on the ship."

When he looks over at Sam, Sam gives him a little nod.

I have to admit that I find the fact that the two of them can have a whole conversation without saying a single word a little unnerving.

"The security wasn't so terrible, was it?"

"Not *so* terrible," I say, giving Sam a teasing smile. "He was a good sport about letting us stop for ice cream."

"I'll always let you stop for ice cream."

I step forward, and shake Sam's hand. "It was a pleasure. I apologize for complaining about it at first."

Sam is about to say something, but Caleb cuts him off, giving me a sharp look. "Don't worry. You'll have more time to get used to each other."

Somehow I knew that this wasn't going to be the only time I was going to have Sam's company, but I'm not going to fight Caleb on it.

"Will that be all, Sir?" Sam asks Caleb.

Caleb nods.

"It was nice to meet you, Sam."

"You too, ma'am."

I let out a long-suffering sigh. "I see we're back to this ma'am business. I'm going to break you at some point."

Sam grins at me. "I look forward to it."

Once Sam is out the front door, I turn to Caleb, who is pulling on his tie. "You're not very friendly with him."

He looks at me as if I've just said the most absurd thing he's ever heard. "I pay him to make sure that nothing bad happens to you, Mia. I don't have to be nice to him for that."

I furrow my brow, and Caleb's expression softens. "It would be nice if you could be nice, that's all I'm saying."

"That's not the way I do business, Mia."

"I'm not telling you how to do business, Caleb," I reply. "It's just an observation, that's all."

He takes a deep breath, then unbuttons his cufflinks and starts rolling up his sleeves. "Noted. You had fun today?"

"Yes!" I reply, nodding. "I like Felicity a *lot.*"

Caleb grins fondly. "Me too."

"I'm glad that you set up our little clothing expedition. I've never really enjoyed shopping, until today."

"And it looks like you were successful," he says, pointing at the mountain of bags.

"We were." I take a step forward, stretch on my tip toes, and kiss him. "Thank you. That doesn't seem like enough, but…*thank you.* I didn't know how much I needed a day out." A safe day out, is what I really mean. Even though I fought Caleb over sending Sam along with us, I'm glad he was there. He allowed me to enjoy myself out in public in a way that I haven't since I left Chicago.

"You don't have to thank me," Caleb replies. "But if you really want to do something nice, have dinner with me."

"That sounds like it'll be nice for me, too."

He takes my hand, and plants a kiss across my knuckles. "Here's hoping."

~

When Caleb asked me if I would have dinner with him, I assumed he wanted me to put on one of my new dresses, and join him at some restaurant that had a months-long waiting list, where he'd be able to walk right up to the hostess and get a table. I was not expecting him to take my hand, lead me into the kitchen, and pull out one of the barstools. I definitely wasn't expecting him to open the fridge and start pulling out ingredients.

"What's going on here?" I ask, mostly teasing, but still kind of confused.

Caleb gives me a mischievous grin. "I'm making you dinner."

"That's why you rolled up your sleeves?" I say, as I pour two glasses of wine.

"Mmm-hmm. I mean business."

"Here I thought you were trying to turn me on."

Caleb laughs as he walks to the other side of the kitchen. "There is no trying as far as that's concerned." He winks before he disappears into the pantry, the smug bastard.

When Caleb comes out, he puts the items that he's carrying down onto the countertop, one by one. He looks at me, gauging my reaction to the weirdest group of ingredients I've ever seen in my life.

"You're using bread, hazelnut spread, apples, and…what is

that? Cheddar? Is that all…going together?"

"This is freshly baked bread, I'll have you know."

"Baked by whom?" Surely Caleb did not bake this bread himself.

"By a lovely woman who mans the oven at one of the best bakeries on the Upper West Side. I bought the cheddar this afternoon from the cheesemonger, and the hazelnut spread came from a gourmet shop down the street."

"Ooooh," I say, trying to sound impressed and not as grossed out as I feel looking at the ingredients for what is sure to be an interesting dinner. "What about the apples?"

Caleb shrugs. "I have no idea where those came from."

"And you're going to let them taint this *gourmet* concoction that you're gonna cook up?" It's a last-ditch effort at goading him into not making whatever it is that he's about to make. "Are you sure you don't want to go to an orchard in Connecticut? Pick some fresh, organic apples?"

A slow smile blooms on his lips, and for a second I think I might be successful here, but then he pulls out a cutting board and knife. "Nope, these will do *just* fine."

Okay, so, there's no getting out of this. I'm looking forward to watching Caleb make whatever it is he's about to make, I'm not so sure about eating it.

"Do you have an apron, or are you just going to risk getting that nice shirt dirty."

"I'll have you know that I *do* have an apron," he says,

teasing. “Well, I *did* have one. Felicity gave it to me as a joke.”

“What was the joke?”

“That I don’t know how to cook. The apron caught on fire when I leaned over a burner once.”

I stifle my laugh with the back of my hand. “Yeah, that’s generally not a good idea.”

“Unfortunately I found that out the hard way.”

“You know, telling me you’re a bad cook isn’t doing much to inspire confidence in this particular meal. Especially not with the ingredient list.”

“I may not be a good cook, but this? This is my specialty,” he says, opening the loaf of bread. He pulls a bread knife out of a drawer and begins slicing it. “And you’re gonna love it.”

“How, exactly, did a terrible cook like you get a specialty?” I ask, sliding his glass of wine across the island, so it sits in front of him.

He puts four slides of bread to the side, and finds a smaller knife in the drawer beside him. He cuts a few small slices into one of the apples, and says, “My mom used to make it for me. It was the only thing she knew how to cook herself.” There’s a wistful smile on his face, and it makes my heart ache. Even if Felicity hadn’t let the information about his parents slip earlier, I would’ve known there was a painful story behind this dinner. “Our cook taught me when I was a teenager. I don’t make it very often, but…” he shrugs, and I know that’s as far as the story is going to go tonight.

I could very easily look up information about Caleb's family on the internet. Once I found out his last name, I discovered some cursory things, but I didn't go digging very far. I figure he was at a distinct disadvantage between the two of us. Since Caleb is rich and has put together some fairly lucrative business deals, it isn't hard to get the scoop on his past and his life. I'm not so easy to find on the internet, so I figured I'd level the playing filed by not looking up anything about him. Whatever I know about him is going to come from him (or, after this afternoon, his friends). No cheating.

"I'm sure I'll love it," I tell him. And I'm not even placating him this time. "So, what exactly is this sandwich?"

He spreads butter on the bread he's sliced. "It's hazelnut spread, cheddar, and sliced apples. Kind of like an exotic grilled cheese."

The thought of it isn't exactly appealing, but I'm gonna give it a try.

"My mom's specialty was club crackers and fake cheese," I tell him with a smile. "I'll save you from that one."

Caleb arches his brow. "Fake cheese?"

"Yeah," I tell him, sliding my finger along the edge of the stem of my wine glass. "Processed cheese? Fake? The kind that's really orange and delicious?"

"I'm not familiar with it."

"Oh, well...Maybe I won't save you from that one after all. It's not a dinner, more like a snack."

"I'd love to try it," he says, grinning at me.

"You might wish you hadn't felt that way after you do," I reply, laughing.

Caleb turns and opens a few cabinet doors, looking for a pan, maybe. I find it funny that the man has no idea how to cook, yet spent who knows how much money on remodeling this place with top-of-the-line appliances, and the nicest cabinets and countertops I've ever seen in person. I know there's a certain mindset that makes you want the best when you can afford it, but it amuses me that he doesn't even know where his pans are. Pans that I'm sure are top-of-the-line, too.

Him cooking for me is a sweet gesture, made sweeter by the fact that he's making something for me that reminds him of his mother. I'd take something intimate and personal like this over a thousand fancy dinners, and it occurs to me that I should probably make something for him some day soon. Considering I actually know how to use all this mind-blowingly amazing equipment. I make a mental note to find out what some of his favorite foods are; maybe I'll surprise him one night when I know he's had a long day at the office.

Caleb finally finds the pan he was looking for, and I watch him as he carefully assembles the sandwiches, a small smile on his face all the while. I get a pretty nice view when he turns his back to me to put the sandwiches in the pan, and I lean back in my chair and enjoy the view while I sip on the rest of my glass of wine.

Once the sandwiches are cooked, he takes the time to plate them neatly. I have to admit, these smell pretty good. They look pretty good, too.

He puts a handful of chips on one plate, and then the other. "These are homemade," he tells me proudly.

"In whose home?" I tease.

He reaches over and takes the chips off of my plate and heaps them on to his.

"Hey!" I reply, reaching over and snagging one before he can pull his plate away.

"Make fun of the cook, and this is what you get!"

He's grinning as he walks around the island and takes his seat next to me.

"Okay," he says, rubbing his hands together. "Tell me what you think."

I take a bite. I have to smile, because as weird as I thought it would be, this sandwich? It's amazing.

"Good?" he asks, practically sitting on the edge of his seat, waiting for my reaction.

"Delicious," I tell him honestly.

"Yeah?"

I nod enthusiastically. "Yeah."

He turns in his chair, ready to eat, and I can see that he's just so pleased. Happiness is radiating off of him, and I think it's the cutest thing I've ever seen.

"Hey," I say, sliding my hand up his shoulder.

When I lean over and kiss him, he smiles against my lips.

"Thank you for sharing this with me." The sandwich, the story behind it. Everything.

He cups my cheek and says, "You're welcome."

CHAPTER *Twenty*

When it's dark outside, and I'm in Caleb's bed, lying in his arms, it's easy to forget about everything that exists outside of the walls of this apartment. It's difficult not to get lost in him, in the way he makes me feel when he touches me, the hot brand of his lips against my skin. Even when we're apart, I remember the way the soft scratch of his chin feels against the crook of my neck when he nuzzles in and kisses me there.

I think about the way it feels when Caleb holds me, when he cradles me against his body. To say that I'm missing him right now is an understatement. Sure, he's right *here* but my whole body is aching for him. We haven't had sex since before I was robbed, and I miss the weight of him on top of me. I miss the way my thigh muscles stretch when I'm straddling him. I miss the feeling of him inside me, and the way his body stiffens and his face goes slack as he calls out my name when he comes.

To say I'm desperate for him would be putting it mildly.

That's why I'm kissing my way along his chest, licking his abs, and nibbling on his skin. My hands are everywhere, and Caleb has—thankfully—not turned me down yet, although there's this niggling fear in the back of my mind that he's going to do that the very second I give him a chance to come to his senses. Good thing I don't plan on giving him that kind of chance.

He's really into it, and pretty far gone, from what I can tell. His chest is rumbling with quiet sounds of pleasure, and his fingers are threaded through my hair, cupping the back of my head.

When I slide my hand down to grip his cock, that's when I know I've taken this a little too far, a little too fast.

He stiffens, and not in the good way.

"Mia," he says reluctantly. His voice is tight, like he's doing everything in his power to keep a tight leash on his control.

"Don't tell me that we can't," I warn, and I keep kissing my way across his body.

"We can't. Not yet."

I lean up on my elbows, so I can look him in his lust-filled eyes when I plead my case. "My head is fine, Caleb. You're not going to fuck me into a concussion."

The backs of his fingers tenderly slide across my still

swollen cheek. He's hesitating a little, considering my argument. I've got him turned on enough that it's probably difficult for him to remember all the reasons he's convinced himself that we shouldn't be doing this. The way he's looking at my cheek, though…that's when it hits me.

I roll off of him—onto my back—and desperately try to make the sting of tears behind my eyes disappear. I don't want to cry in front of him, that's not fair.

"I get it," I say, rubbing at my eyes. "Me looking like this isn't hot for you."

"Mia," he replies gently. "No. That's not it. I don't care what you look like, I…look at me. Will you look at me, please?"

I roll over onto my side, and reluctantly my gaze finds his. He gives me a gentle smile, then presses his lips against mine.

"You're beautiful, and I want you. I think that much is fairly obvious." He gestures at his groin, and I can't help but laugh. "Just…I'll feel better if we wait a day or two. Can you do that for me?"

Caleb pulls me in, snuggling me against his chest. "Yeah," I say, trying to hide my disappointment. "I can do that."

"I'll make it worth the wait." His voice is all low and seductive, and it's really not fair.

"Don't tease me if you're not going to follow through."

"Fair enough," Caleb says, and I can hear his smile in his voice. He shifts our bodies so that we're both lying on our sides. His legs settle behind mine, and he wraps his arm around my waist and pulls me back against him, cuddling my head beneath his chin.

"We can do other things, you know," he says, planting a kiss on my neck.

"Don't tease me." I sound irritated as I swat at his arm, and I am. I'm so irritated with him for not having sex with me, that it makes me even more irritated that he thinks he can just kiss me like that without the promise of something more.

"I'm sorry." He twines our fingers together, and says, "Tell me something about you."

"That's one way to derail things," I reply, laughing.

He gives me a squeeze. "C'mon. Tell me."

"Like what?"

"Like...something I don't know."

Oh, there's so much he doesn't know about me, and if I tell him any of the most recent big developments in my life, he's going to push me out of his strong, warm arms. He's going to ask me to leave his bed, his apartment, and his life. He's clearly feeling a little sentimental today, after making me dinner and sharing the story about his mother with me. It makes me want to share some of the things I hold dear with him, although I think that's a conversation that I'm going to have to ease my way into.

Maybe I should start small, and see where this goes from there.

"When I was a kid, I had a pet rabbit named Piglet."

Caleb laughs, making my hair flutter across my cheek. "Sounds appropriate."

"I've never been appropriate," I say, pressing my ass against him. He growls against my ear as a warning, but that's what he gets for teasing me. "What else?"

"Anything you want to tell me."

I grin, because I know him well enough to know that he's definitely after something, but is unsure about outright asking the question. Just to assure him that I'm not feeling defensive or anything, I give his arm a little squeeze before I say, "You should go ahead and ask me what you'd like to know. I know you're doing a little fishing here."

He lets out a small sigh, and I'm not quite sure what that means. It takes a few moments before he finally speaks.

"You told me that your parents are dead, back when you were in the hospital. It was right after you woke up, so I'm not sure if you remember."

"I remember," I say.

"I was hoping you'd bring it up at some point, and I didn't want to pry, but I've been thinking about it ever since."

I can certainly understand why, after finding out this afternoon that his parents are dead, too. It's only natural that he'd be curious, and I respect the fact that he didn't want to pry, much like I don't want to. I also appreciate that he asked me instead of going looking for the information. It's certainly out there. Well, it's out there for my father, at least.

"You don't have to tell me about it if you don't want to," he says, nuzzling against my hair. "I know I'm bringing it up out of nowhere."

"Not nowhere," I assure him. "I figured you'd ask me about it at some point, and to be honest, if you'd waited for me to bring it up myself, I'm...well, I don't know how long that would've taken."

"It can take as long as you need it to," he says, and I believe him.

I know that he's curious—he wouldn't have asked me about this if he wasn't—but there isn't a doubt in my mind that if I tell him that I'd rather not talk about this tonight, that it would be okay. I'm not ready to tell him everything; I'm especially wary of telling him about my father. It's almost impossible to tell that story without getting into why I'm here now, so I'm going to offer up a compromise.

"Can I just...Is it okay if I just talk about my mother?" I ask hesitantly.

Caleb kisses my head. "Of course. You don't-"

"I want to," I tell him.

"Okay."

"I look a lot like her," I begin, as Caleb's fingertips begin a soothing circuit up and down my forearm. "She had a fearlessness about her that just...it isn't part of my make up. Sadly, I don't remember a whole lot about her. She died when I was very young." I don't want to get into how she died;

sometimes I can still hear the screeching of the tires on the hot asphalt, and the sickening crunch of twisting metal as the truck broadsided our car. "Most of what I remember about her are like…these memories dangling on strings that are just out of my reach. Sometimes I'm able to grab them before they float away, but sometimes they disappear. Like, I have clear memories of her having cheese and crackers waiting for me as a snack when I came home from school.

"Most of my memories of her are more like…feelings, if that makes sense. Sometimes I'll walk into a room and I'll smell her perfume, and I get these butterflies in my stomach, and I feel…*safe*. Or, I'll see a woman who I think looks like her from behind, and for a moment I'll forget that she's dead, and in that moment? I'm happy. Sometimes I find myself humming the melody that she used to sing when she was cleaning up my scraped knee, and I just know that everything's going to be okay. I know it sounds cheesy, but…"

Caleb holds me tight. "It doesn't sound cheesy at all. What was the melody?"

I close my eyes, take a deep breath, and hum a few bars of the song. My voice is wobbly, and I'm probably not getting it entirely right, but this part stands out the brightest in my memory.

"You must have really missed her growing up," he says, his voice tinged with the kind of sadness that someone only has when they understand exactly what you've been through.

"I did." It would have been nice to have her around when I got my first period, when I had my first kiss. It feels selfish to feel sadness over missing those things with her, but I do. "My dad did his best, though. We lived next door to a single mother and her son, and she always treated me like I was one of her own. I was lonely a lot, but…having them made it better." When I think of Amelia—Marcus's mother—I feel my breath catch in my throat. I'm reminded that I haven't called him since my accident. I need to do that, or he'll start wondering if Privya caught up with me. Even though I have to be pretty vague with him during our calls, I don't want him panicking.

"I'm glad you had someone like that in your life," Caleb whispers.

"I'm glad I did, too. I think the family you make is just as important as the one you're born into."

Caleb and I are already pressed pretty tightly together, but he somehow manages to wrap himself around me. He slides his thigh between mine, and rests his chin on the top of my head. Even though he's definitely the big spoon in this scenario I get the feeling that I'm offering him way more support than he's offering me.

The air around us stills in that way that it tends to, like something big is coming and you're just waiting for it to arrive. There's actual weight in the room, hovering just above us, and Caleb is getting ready to let it drop.

"My parents died in a plane crash," he tells me. His voice is softer and more vulnerable than I've ever heard it before, and I know it's taking a lot for him to share this with me.

I give his hand a gentle, reassuring squeeze. He gave me the courtesy of letting me work through my confession without commentary, so I'm going to do the same thing for him. Another, less selfless part of me, is afraid that if I say something, he'll stop talking.

"They were on a trip," he says. His voice is a little stronger now. "It was work related; my dad was trying to shore up some merger, and my mom had gone with him because she wanted to do some shopping in San Francisco. It was the day before my sixteenth birthday. They had bought me this amazing Porsche that I had been dying for, and they couldn't wait to give me the keys. I know it makes me sound like such a spoiled little rich kid."

"It does not," I assure him. Okay, it does a little, but I can't even imagine the Caleb that I know now as a spoiled teenaged brat. If his parents wanted him to have that car, it's because they thought he deserved it, and he shouldn't feel bad about that.

"My dad and I were supposed to go golfing in the morning," he tells me. "It was a Simmons family sixteenth birthday tradition. My mom was going to make us brunch. Those sandwiches were the only things she knew how to make. It was the one day a year that she ever cooked anything for us, and I always looked forward to it.

"One of my dad's meetings ran late, and there was an issue with the plane. A mechanic spent all day working on repairs, and assured my parents that everything was in good working order. My dad didn't even give it a second thought, because he wanted to get home before tee time, and they were already cutting it so close.

"They ran into engine trouble somewhere over Colorado. The pilot wasn't able to compensate when one of the engines went out."

"Caleb," I whisper. Despite the hold he has on me, I manage to turn myself around in his arms, so we're lying face-to-face. I place my hand on his cheek, and it seems to calm him some.

"I hated that fucking Porsche," he says with a sad smile. "My dad's butler gave me the keys a few days after the funeral, and told me how excited he was for me to have it. I knew my father well, and even though I *know* he would've trusted the mechanic's word that everything was fixed regardless, part of me will always wonder if he would've held off on leaving if he and my mother hadn't been trying so desperately to get home on time."

"You can't think like that," I tell him, pressing a soft kiss to his lips.

"I know I can't. I…I got drunk that night, when I got the keys. I got drunk and I drove, like a fucking asshole, and wrapped that car around a telephone pole. I went to live with Ben and his family until I turned eighteen. They treated me like one of their own kids, too. They always had. I'm lucky that I had them, but…sometimes I felt alone, too. So I know what that's like."

I feel tears pricking at the back of my eyes, because Caleb is such a loving and caring man. I can't even picture a world without him in it. He's only been a part of my life for a month, and he's…he's irreplaceable.

"We spent so much time alone," I tell him, before placing another kiss on his lips. I feel sorry for the younger versions of us, crippled by loss and unable to really share it with anyone. But those losses led us here, so some good came out of them after all.

"Not anymore," he says softly.

"Not anymore."

CHAPTER Twenty-One

I'm sitting at the island in Caleb's kitchen, surrounded by several different varieties of gourmet bagels, and a selection of artisan cream cheese spreads from one of my favorite bakeries down the street. A steaming hot mocha, made just the way I like it, is warming my right hand.

In retrospect, I should've known that Caleb was trying to butter me up for something.

My mouth is hanging open, which I'm sure makes me look absolutely ridiculous. It takes me a minute to find my bearings, but when I do, all I'm capable of saying is, "You want me to go to a *ball*?"

Caleb laughs, shaking his head as he dips the end of his knife into a tub of garden vegetable cream cheese. "It's not a ball, it's a benefit."

My eyebrows scrunch together. "Is…is there a difference?"

Caleb has been pretty patient with me thus far, but he's starting to look at me like I have two heads or something. Like the answer to this question should be obvious. "Balls are held for a bunch of rich, pompous windbags who get together to dance and eat insanely expensive food, and stand around and congratulate each other about how rich they all are."

"Well," I say, blowing into the small opening on the lid of my cup to cool down my coffee. "That doesn't sound appealing at all."

"*Benefits*," he replies pointedly, "are held for a bunch of rich, pompous windbags who get together to dance and eat insanely expensive food, and stand around and raise money for charity."

I can't help but laugh at his unflattering, probably accurate description. "And you want me to attend this gathering as one of your fellow windbags?"

"Not a fellow windbag." He sounds offended on my behalf. "As the date of a windbag. This windbag," he says, pointing at himself. "I need some arm candy." He grabs his bagel and his coffee, walks around the island, and comes to rest right in front of me.

"Oh, I'm arm candy now, is that right?"

"You're the sweetest arm candy there is." He leans down and kisses me, and I have to admit…it's pretty sweet.

"You're not playing fair, convincing me with a kiss like that."

"There's more where that came from, if you need more convincing."

"Oh yeah?" I say, sounding breathless in a way that would embarrass me, if I cared even a little bit about being embarrassed in front of this man.

"Yeah." Caleb leans in, and presses his lips against my neck, sucking gently in that spot that drives me crazy. Oh, he's good.

Okay, he's kissing me into it. "Is that why you told Felicity to pick out a nice dress for me when we went shopping the other day?"

He hums against my neck, and oh, that's nice. "Maybe," he says, as his lips brush across my skin.

"Sneaky," I reply. "I like it."

Caleb leans back, looking at me with what seems like just a touch of apprehension in his eyes. "My friend Oliver will be there. I'd like you to meet him."

First Ben and Felicity. Now Oliver. He's integrating me into his life more and more, and even though I should probably tap the brakes on this thing, I don't want it to stop.

"Tell me about the food," I say with a grin, as I swipe my fingertip along the edge of my bagel, then lick the little bit of cream cheese off.

"So much food," he says. "Trays and trays of food."

"I'm warming up to this idea," I reply, teasing.

"Tell me what it'll take to get you warmer." Caleb is sliding his hands up and down my arms, and giving me that look that's impossible to say no to. Not that I was ever going to say no in the first place.

"You should probably tell me what will be waiting for me after the benefit."

He furrows his brow, and looks adorably confused. "What's waiting for you after?"

"I mean, what's going to happen after this benefit. You'll be looking amazing in a tux, wearing suspenders, I assume?"

Caleb grins. "Suspenders can definitely be arranged," he says, bracing one hand against the countertop so he can lean in like a gorgeous predator, going in for the kill.

"I'll be wearing a dress."

"Mmm," he hums. "A very sexy dress."

"Low cut," I tell him, skimming my finger down the collar of my tank top. Purely for demonstration purposes. "After the ball-"

"Benefit," he corrects.

I playfully roll my eyes. "After the *benefit*, whatever will you do with me?"

"Oh," he says throatily, his voice dark and deep. "I can think of lots of things."

Mmm. I'm looking forward to them all.

It's surreal to me that I'm standing in the middle of a ballroom that is located in someone's home. A *ballroom*. In someone's *home.* What do they do when they have guests over, and someone asks to use the restroom? Do they say, "Out this door, take a left, and it's the door just past the ballroom"? Sure, this is one of the most upscale buildings in the city, but I never thought there was this kind of real estate inside. I feel like I'm stuck in some grand musical from the fifties or something.

It's not unpleasant, it's just…surreal. Caleb is the only rich person I've ever known, and I thought he could be a little silly with his money, like when he hired a bodyguard to follow me around the city. No, that purchase was practical, and money well-spent. A ballroom? That's just crazy.

Speaking of the bodyguard, Sam's here with us tonight, although I can't imagine why. I didn't have the heart or the wherewithal to fight Caleb on it before we left the house. If it makes him feel better, then I'll go along with it. Besides, there doesn't seem to be a shortage of personal security here tonight, so maybe Caleb brought him along for that reason. Whatever the reasoning, I find that I don't really care. Even though I teased Caleb about coming here, I'm actually having a great time.

Ben and Felicity are in attendance, like Caleb said they would be. Ben has a date that I've only seen once tonight; she seems to be a socialite in her own right, and Ben doesn't seem to be all that interested, so I'm guessing it was a last-minute date. Felicity is here alone, and she's off getting a drink.

Caleb is standing next to me, his hand settled on the small

of my back, where it has been most of the night. I'm not sure if he wants everyone here to know that I'm here with him, or if he just wants to keep a connection with me, to keep me from getting too nervous. Regardless, I like the reassuring feel of his skin on mine. I'm not going to complain about it.

An incredibly attractive man with dark blonde hair and bright blue eyes approaches Caleb and me. He's gorgeous in a rugged way, and the unshaven stubble on his face contrasts with his pressed, polished tuxedo.

"Nice of you to show up," Caleb says, smiling as he reaches out and shakes this man's hand. Based on the pictures that I've seen of this man with Caleb and Ben, I'm assuming this is Oliver.

"Flight got in late," he says with a smile. "You must be Mia." He reaches out and takes my hand. "It's so nice to finally meet you. Caleb talks about you a lot."

I get the feeling that Oliver is gently ribbing Caleb, but when I look over at Caleb I can see that he isn't bothered by it in the least. "I do," he says, grinning.

"It's nice to meet you," I reply, and give his hand a squeeze.

"I hear you two met at one of my properties."

"We did," I confirm. "It was lovely."

Oliver grins at me, and wow. That grin is more than a little breathtaking. It makes him even more handsome, which I wasn't sure was possible.

"Are you talking about the hotel, or meeting Caleb?" he

asks, teasing.

"Both?"

Oliver laughs. "I'm going to take some matchmaking credit there," he says lightly.

"Having fun without me?" Felicity says, before taking a sip of champagne.

Caleb replies, "Never," while Oliver gives Felicity a long, loaded look.

"Hi," she says to him, looking a little coy. Her voice is quiet and shy, and if I didn't know any better, I'd say she was blushing.

Oliver's whole demeanor changes, and he gives her a soft, boyish grin. "Hi."

Oh. *Oh*, there's something between the two of them. Either that, or they desperately want something more. Hmm.

"Mia," Ben says, as he walks up to our little group. "It's good to see you again. You look beautiful tonight."

"Thank you," I reply with a smile. "And speaking of thank you's, I owe you one. The system you built for me is magnificent."

"I know." He's grinning, like any cocky programmer worth his salt would. That makes me like him even more. "I'm happy to do it. I know what it's like to be without something. These three used to make fun of me for always having my laptop on me," he says, motioning toward Caleb, Oliver, and Felicity. "I'd be enraged if someone stole it out from under me. I hope you set up some protocols."

I give him this mock offended look. "Of course I did. The whole system overwrites itself when someone who isn't me tries to log in."

"A woman after my own heart."

"Hey," Caleb interrupts. "You've got your own date, not that you seem to be all that interested."

"Cara called me, I didn't call her," Ben says, trying to defend himself. "This was strictly a business arrangement."

"Oh, the depths she sank to, just so she wouldn't have to walk the press line alone," Oliver says.

"You've been there a time or two before," Felicity teases.

Oliver winks at her, and I can practically see her swoon.

"Ignore them," Ben says to me, pulling me to the side so the others can't hear our conversation. "I know you said you have some projects you're working on, but I meant what I said about wanting to see what you can do. My company has great benefits, and for someone with the kind of coding experience you have, I can surely make it worth your while."

"I'll consider it," I tell him, smiling. I know he must think that I'm playing professionally hard to get, but I'm not. I really do want to consider his offer; I would love long-term gainful employment here, and a chance to work on some large-scale innovative projects. I know this is crazy, and that it's foolishly hopeful, but the longer my tracking program runs without any hits, the safer I feel here. The safer I feel, the more hope starts to creep in where it has no business being. Hope makes me think that maybe I can stay here. Hope tells me that I might be able to make a fresh start in a new city, and outrun all the consequences that are waiting for me back in Chicago.

Hope is a terribly seductive thing.

I turn to Caleb, who is patiently waiting for me to return the to the conversation. Oliver and Felicity are off in their own world, and Ben walked away to find something to eat.

"Hey," I say to Caleb, gently pulling on the sleeve of his jacket to get his attention. I nod in Felicity and Oliver's direction. "Are those two…"

"No," Caleb answers hastily, without even a thought. "No way. Ben would lose it."

I want to tell him that Ben shouldn't have a say in his sister's or his friend's love life, but it's not my business, and I don't want to fight about it.

"One of my investors is over there, mind if I go say hello?" Caleb asks.

Bless him for noticing that my eyes completely glaze over when he's talking business. I nod, and give him a quick kiss before he walks away. Oliver joins him, leaving me alone with Felicity.

"We should head to the powder room," Felicity says. She smiling at me, but she gently grabs my wrist and pulls me through the crowd, so there isn't really time for me to argue with her.

The room is empty, thankfully, and she pulls a compact out of her purse and pats my cheek with it.

"Your bruise was starting to show," she says.

"Oh!" I turn and look in the mirror, where I can see the faint hint of yellowish-green peeking out from under my foundation. "Caleb didn't say anything."

Felicity smiles at me. "I don't think that's what he notices when he looks at you."

I can't help but smile back at her. She's so sweet, and I'm so lucky to have a friend here, someone I can talk to who isn't Caleb.

"Thank you for taking care of me."

"You're welcome," she says, patting my cheek. "Does it hurt?"

"No," I tell her. "Not anymore."

I watch her in silence, until the curiosity is too much. "I'm surprised you noticed the bruise," I say.

"What do you mean?"

"You mentioned Caleb not noticing this when he looks at me, with the way you were looking at Oliver, I'm surprised you noticed this." I make sure to convey that this is all very lighthearted teasing on my part. I don't want her to get defensive, but she and Oliver are incredibly obvious. I don't think she knows this.

Felicity sighs, and there's a wistful look in her eyes. "Oliver doesn't feel that way about me. I'm just his best friend's annoying little sister."

I grin at her, because she so *blind*. "Oh, I'm pretty sure he think about you as more than that, if the way he looks at you is any indication." I wink at her, and she's definitely blushing now.

"There," she says, snapping her compact shut. "Good as new."

She, however, clearly does not want to pursue this conversation, and I'm not going to push her into talking about something she doesn't want to talk about.

"Thank you," I tell her, leaning in for a quick hug.

"Anytime."

I'm finding that despite the fact that I came to New York City not intending to put down any kind of roots, the need to make a friendship grow with Felicity is pretty strong. She's a lovely person, and I like being around her. I like *who I am* when I'm around her.

"Feel like getting together for lunch later this week?" I ask.

She beams at me as she slides her compact back into her clutch. "I'd love that."

CHAPTER Twenty-Two

"You looked beautiful in that dress, but you look even better out of it," Caleb says, as he kisses and licks his way across my chest. We're both naked and in his bed, and it's like coming home again, because it's been way too long since we've been together like this.

My fingers slide through his soft hair, and I smile. For the past week and a half, ever since the robbery, it's like we've been living in a world where everything is tilted just slightly to the right. Now, lying naked in each other's arms, with Caleb's hot mouth trailing slow, wet kisses across my skin, it feels like the world is starting to make sense again.

"I wish you would have kept the suspenders on, honestly. Actually, you should still be wearing the whole ensemble."

Caleb chuckles, as he licks a circle around my nipple, then tugs it between his teeth. "You don't like me naked?"

"I love you naked. You should be naked almost all the time."

"Almost?" Another, more teasing bite to my nipple.

"We should've had a quickie in the back of the car, is what I'm saying."

"Why didn't you mention that?" he asks, as his lips continue their incredibly pleasant assault on my body. He lifts his head, his eyebrows furrowed together. "Hell, why didn't *I* think of that?"

"Maybe you were distracted by me," I say, arching my back to give me more contact with him. "I know I was distracted by thoughts of you doing what you're doing right now."

That answer makes him move to my other breast and continue the kissing and licking with even more enthusiasm. "So, you were too distracted by the thought of having sex to think of having sex?"

"Well…yes."

He laughs, as his hand slides down the side of my thigh. "One of the many things I love about you."

Somewhere, in the part of my brain that isn't completely filled with lust and thoughts of sex, I register that Caleb just said the L-word, but I'm too wrapped up in all the things that he's doing to my body to be able to focus on it. If I try to focus on anything other than what he's doing to my body, I'm 99% sure that my brain will short circuit a little bit. Besides, loving something about someone isn't the same as actually loving them. Those are two different things, so I'm not even going to dedicate any of my precious brainpower to dwelling on it.

"I was also thinking about doing this," I tell him, gently pushing on his abs. "Lie back."

With a wicked grin, Caleb does exactly as I ask. He knows what I'm going to do; the anticipation of it is written all over his face, and in the taught pull of his muscles. He loves it when I suck his dick, and it's been far too long for both of us. He settles himself against the pillows, looking like some kind of artfully arranged Adonis. His body is just unfair, but I can't deny the fact that I feel incredibly lucky that I'm the one who gets to see him like this, to make him feel so, so good. I know there are countless women who would love to be in my place, and I don't take that for granted.

With a gentle scratch, I slide my nails down his abs. He's irresistible like this—hard body and harder cock—and I just can't keep my hands off of him. I maneuver myself between his legs, and when I get myself situated in a comfortable position, I slide my hands up the insides of his thighs. His muscles tighten, like he's doing whatever he can to hang onto his control.

I'm going to see just how far I can push him tonight.

"What are you doing?" he asks, voice tight.

"You know what I'm doing," I say. I'm making a concerted effort to touch him everywhere but the place he wants it most.

"You're teasing me, that's what."

I laugh as I grip his hard length, sliding my hand up and down. He lets out a sigh of relief when he feels my touch, and he lifts his hips, looking for friction, needing more than just my short, slow strokes.

"Mia," he says. It's like he's pleading and growling all at once. "Put your mouth on my cock."

I love it when he's vocal about what he wants, and when he's a little bit bossy about it. I do what he says, as I lean down and lick a long strip along the underside of his shaft, then swirl my tongue around the head. Caleb lifts his head so he can watch, and his eyelids are heavy with lust. He reaches down and threads his fingers through my hair. He'd never force my head down, but I know he wants me to take him into my mouth.

So, I do. I swirl my tongue around him, alternating sucking and licking. I grip his base with my hand, alternating the movement of my hand and my mouth. He's making these short, low grunts with every move I make, and his breath is coming in quick, hard pants. I keep eye contact with him as I lick and tease more noises out of him. It's almost like a game with myself, wondering what kind of noises my mouth will coax out of him.

"I love your mouth," he says, and I show him just how skilled my mouth is. "Fuck. *Deeper*."

I take him in as deep as I can, then swallow around the tip of his cock as I give his balls a gentle tug. He's propped up on one elbow now, his head thrown back, Adam's apple bobbing as strangled sounds escape his mouth. The bed sheet is twisted between his fingers, and he's trembling with the sheer force of will it takes not to thrust up into my mouth.

I sit back for a moment, needing to catch my breath from the sheer intensity of it all, and in one quick motion, Caleb lifts me up so that I'm draped across his chest. Our mouths crash together, and he kisses me slowly, all desperate and deep.

"Get up on your knees," he says, his lips moving against mine. "Get up on your knees and hold onto the headboard."

It's obvious that Caleb knows that I get turned on when he tells me what to do in bed, and I always respond enthusiastically. He rustles around behind me, probably putting on a condom, and the mattress dips as he situates himself behind me. His thighs bracket mine, and his skin is so incredibly warm. One of his hands slides up my side, until he's cupping my right breast, and he rubs my nipple between his index finger and thumb. With his free hand, he gathers my hair and lays it over my left shoulder, then latches onto my neck as he thrusts up inside of me.

I arch my back, pulling him in deeper. "Oh god," I say, letting my head fall back against his shoulder.

"Relax into me," he says, wrapping his arms around my chest and middle. "I've got you." Caleb keeps moving his hips relentlessly, and he reaches down to rub at my clit. The spot he's hitting inside of me is *amazing.*

"Do you feel how perfect this is?" he asks. "Me inside of you?"

I can't seem to manage any words, so I just nod. Yes, it's perfect.

"We were made for each other," he says, his voice low and deep as he nips at my earlobe.

"Harder," I beg. "Please."

I don't have to ask Caleb twice. He trusts into me harder, faster, to the point where our skin slaps together with every move he makes. Again, and again, and again, never slowing, driving me further and further into pleasure until I'm falling apart, clenching around him. He holds onto me tight, then he falls after me, faltering as he rides out his orgasm, saying my name.

We both ride out the aftershocks together, moving a little, rocking against each other. Caleb kisses his way across my back, and his lips feel good against my sweat-slicked skin.

"I'm falling in love with you," he whispers, nuzzling his nose into my hair.

It's the kind of thing someone says in the hazy aftermath of a great orgasm; maybe it's the truth, and maybe it isn't. Either way, I'm not going to hold him to it.

But the thing is…I'm falling in love with him, too.

CHAPTER Twenty-Three

The smell of freshly brewed coffee drags me out of what was an incredibly restful slumber. When I open my eyes, the lack of Caleb's body snuggling up to mine alerts me that I'm alone in the bed. I slide my arm out, touching Caleb's side, and the sheets are still warm. After I slide out of bed, I pad over to the dresser, and pull out one of Caleb's shirts. I know he likes to see me in them, and it's a lazy Sunday morning. Chances are, he won't even turn on his laptop to do a little work until later this afternoon.

I'm hoping for a repeat performance of last night, and walking out to greet Caleb dressed like this is a sure-fire way to get things going in that direction.

I follow the scent of the coffee, and make my way out into the kitchen. Caleb is standing at the kitchen island, a pair of sweatpants slung low on his hips, and his hair is all tousled from sleep. He's shirtless, just the way I like him, and he's skimming through the Business section of the newspaper. It's nice, waking up to a warm cup of coffee poured by someone like Caleb. It's more than I deserve, but I'm going to appreciate every moment of it while I can.

He looks up, as if he can sense that I'm looking at him.

"Hey," he says sleepily, smiling at me.

I can see the moment he recognizes what I'm wearing, and the happiness in his eyes melts away into something more carnal.

He slides a cup across the island; it's still so hot that it's steaming.

"Hey," I reply, making my way over to where that liquid gold is waiting for me. It's got cream and a teaspoon of sugar in it, just the way I like it, and a strong rush of affection for this man hits me square in the chest. "Thank you for this."

Caleb reaches across the island, and takes hold of the mug's handle. "If you want more, you're gonna have to come and get it."

I do want more, so I go and get it. Caleb warps his arm around my waist, and pulls me close, giving me a soft kiss. "Good morning."

"Good morning," I reply.

Caleb hands me my coffee, and I take a long sip, letting out an appreciative noise when I swallow.

"Your laptop was going off a few minutes ago," he says

casually.

I narrow my eyes at him. "Going off?"

"Yeah," he says, turning a page of the paper. "Beeping. I hope you don't mind, but I muted it. I went to wake you up, but you looked so peaceful in bed."

A cold chill runs down my spine, and my grip just…gives out. The coffee cup I'm holding falls to the floor, splashing hot coffee all over my legs. I'm too stunned and panicked to even care about the pain.

"Jesus, Mia," Caleb says, sounding worried.

I vaguely register him moving in my peripheral vision, and then he's kneeling in front of me, wiping the coffee off of my legs with a hand towel.

"Are you okay?" he asks. "Mia?"

The panic in his voice is increasing with the panic in my chest. I turn, and walk over to where my laptop is sitting on the dining room table. Sure enough, my tracking program is up, only instead of alerts for Privya's name or whereabouts, I see my own name. Multiple times. I had set up a search for myself, just in case, and it started going off really early this morning. When I click on one of the alerts, the link takes me to the website for a gossip rag. There's a picture posted of me and Caleb from last night.

How did anyone at that site find out my name? Was I on a guest list somewhere? Did Caleb, or Felicity, or maybe Ben tell someone? Why did I even tell them my real name? I checked in to the hotels with aliases. Why...why did I let them in? Does any of this even matter now? My name is out there. My face is out there, and I've just given someone who knows where to look a map that leads straight to me.

It also leads straight to Caleb.

Fuck.

"Is everything okay?" Caleb asks cautiously from the doorway. He's looking at me like I'm a wild animal that he's scared to spook.

Before I answer him that no, everything might not be okay, I need to know how not okay things are. I check the alerts that I have set up on Privya, and there aren't any. Not yet. Either he's not on the move, or he's been using cash, like me. Or he's traveling in some other kind of way that I'm unable to trace. Regardless, nothing that I have access to gives me any indication that he's left Chicago.

So, I've got that going for me, I guess.

"Everything's okay," I tell Caleb. My voice is shaky, though, and I know he'll catch the lie. Sometimes the man can read me like a book.

He walks up behind me, and I jump when he touches my shoulder. "Mia?"

"It's noth-"

"Don't tell me this is nothing," he says. The panic in his voice earlier is being overtaken by anger. It's burning around the edges, just waiting to catch fire. "Tell me the truth."

I walk over to the floor-to-ceiling windows, and look out at the park. For so long, being in this apartment let me forget about the outside world. Right now, I'd love to be out in it. I'd love to be anywhere but here. This is the moment that I let myself believe would never come.

This is the moment that proves I'm a fool.

"God damn it, Mia," Caleb says, walking up behind me. "Your computer's going off like crazy, you dropped your coffee all over yourself and barely even noticed it. You look like you've seen a ghost. Tell me what the fuck is going on. Now."

Caleb's patience has run out, and I don't blame him for not wanting to wait anymore. Honestly, I don't want to keep this secret anymore. So, here goes.

"It's true what I told you, that I left Chicago because I needed a new start. But needing a new start, it wasn't a voluntary thing," I say, turning my head to the side. I can't bear to look at him, settling instead for seeing him out of the corner of my eye. "I was running away from something there."

"Running away from what?" He walks closer, and I turn my head to look out the window again. Talking is easier this way, because I don't have to see the anger and disappointment on his face. "What are you hiding from me?"

I swallow, not quite sure how I'm going to phrase the next part of the story.

"Look at me," Caleb says roughly.

I do as he asks, I at least owe him that. When my eyes

finally meet his, there's anger there, yes...but there's also fear.

"I've been patient, and I never want to push you, Mia. But if there was ever a time to push, it seems like it's now. I've opened my home to you, and helped you when you didn't have anyone, and you owe me the goddamn truth."

"I know," I say, feeling my eyes water. "I know I do. I wanted to tell you sooner-"

"Bullshit," he says. "If you wanted to tell me sooner, you would've told me sooner."

"I was scared," I admit. My voice sounds smaller than it ever has before, and something in it makes Caleb's expression soften.

He takes a step toward me. "You don't have to be scared with me."

"I do," I say, nodding. The tears are flowing freely now, and I'm not even going to try to stop them. "Once I tell you, you're not going to look at me the way that you do, and I didn't want to lose that. You make me...you make me forget all of this shit, and..."

"I can help you," he says. "But I can't do that if you won't tell me what's wrong."

"You can't help me with this."

Caleb runs his fingers through his hair frustratedly. "You can at least let me try!"

"Can we sit down?"

"I'm fine where I am. Stop trying to stall, Mia."

"Can we please sit down? I'd feel better if we were sitting down."

Caleb lets out a long, shaky breath, and makes his way over to the couch, and sits down. His legs are wide open, his elbows resting on his knees. His foot bounces up and down nervously, like he just can't sit still. He looks as on edge as I feel.

I take a seat on the coffee table across from him. I figure it'll be good to keep some distance between us. I'd feel better if I was wearing something other than Caleb's shirt to have this conversation, but there's no turning back now.

"I don't know where to start," I admit. Do I start by telling him about the money I stole? Do I start at the point when I left Chicago? How far back should I go?

"What were you running away from?" Caleb asks.

"It's complicated."

He sighs, and shrugs his shoulders. "I've got all day, Mia."

I take a deep breath. Here goes.

"I told you the other night about the woman—Amelia—who treated me like one of her own after my mom died."

Caleb nods, acknowledging that he remembers.

"After my mom died, my dad, he was really depressed. He did the best that he could with me, but he didn't really know how to be a single father at first. I guess most people don't, when it comes unexpectedly like that. He was out of work for a while…well, a long while, and we didn't really have that much money to begin with. We had been renting this house in the suburbs—white picket fence and all that—but he couldn't bare to live there anymore with my mom gone, and we couldn't afford the rent, anyway.

"We moved to a…a not-so-nice area of town. My mom was always worried about my education; she wanted me to have the best. So, we lived in this shitty, hole-in-the-wall apartment, and every penny my dad had to spare went to private school tuition. When I'd get home from school in the afternoon, Amelia would invite me over, and she'd make sure I had dinner, because my dad was always working nights. She had a son, Marcus. He and I have been best friends ever since."

"I don't understand what this has to do with you being in some kind of trouble, Mia."

I sigh. "I told you it was complicated. I'm trying to make it as uncomplicated as possible."

"Okay," he breathes. "Okay."

"This building, it was in terrible shape. It was run-down, in disrepair, and it was owned by this shady businessman who was rich as hell, but owned a lot of slummy buildings that he rented to people who were down on their luck, or who couldn't afford to live anywhere else. He cut corners all the time, but sometimes things would be broken for months before he'd get around to hiring a repair man, if he ever even bothered to do that. We filed formal complaints with the city, but this guy had so many officials in his pocket that none of the complaints ever made a difference. It's amazing what money can do to make people turn the other way when you're not doing the right thing."

Caleb's eyes widen, like I actually smacked him, then he looks down at his hands. I reach out and clasp his hand with mine.

"Hey," I tell him. "I don't mean-"

"I know," he replies, and he gives me a halfhearted smile. "It's true, what you said."

"I went off to college in Massachusetts, on a full scholarship. I didn't get home often—we didn't have spare money for the airfare—but when I graduated last year, I moved back to Chicago to be closer to him. The building had really gone to hell. I tried to convince him to let me move us out to a nicer place, but he wouldn't have it. I mean, I couldn't have afforded much better at the time…I was just picking up clients, but I could've afforded better than that."

Caleb is gradually moving closer, leaning into me. I'm guessing he's starting to think that maybe this story isn't as bad as he anticipated, but I'm just now getting there. He's cradling my hand in his now, rubbing his thumbs in a soothing circuit across my wrist.

"I saw news of the explosion on the television," I begin with a sniffle. "I was meeting with a potential client in a cafe. I looked up, and I just…I was in shock. It seems as if my dad died right away. I hope he did, at least. Amelia, she was on her way home from the grocery store, so she didn't take the brunt of the impact, but she had burns all over her body. They ruled it a faulty gas line, but…we complained about so much shit in that building over the years. It was due to neglect, I know it was, but the owner—Jack Kemp—he was pretty much untouchable."

"Your friend Marcus, was he-"

"No," I reply, shaking my head. "No, he wasn't there. Anyway, Kemp gave our families a small stipend. It was enough for me to pay for my dad's funeral, but not much else, considering we had lost everything. There were a few survivors of the blast, but they died within a few days after the explosion. Amelia, she's the only one who survived.

"Unfortunately for her, she didn't have any insurance, and what little help Marcus and I were able to find for her wasn't enough to cover her through the end of her treatment, if there ever *is* an end of her treatment. It had only been four months when I…did what I did, and her bills were already more than she could ever pay. Her apartment blew up; everything she had was gone, and she'd never be able to get out of that debt. How can a person lose everything twice?

"A few ambulance chasers came to Marcus, wanting him to sue, but the terms were more beneficial to them than they would've been to Amelia and Marcus, and Kemp has enough money to tie a case up in court for years, and it might not have even gone their way when it was all said and done. She needed to be moved to a specialized care facility, and she and Marcus needed the money now, not five years from now, or whenever a settlement would be reached."

A look of understanding flits across Caleb's face, melting away whatever anger was left.

"Christ, Mia. You stole the money?"

I lower my head, and nod. I can't look him in the eye, I'm too ashamed.

"And Marcus let you?"

The shame I was feeling dissolves quickly, and I look up, glaring at Caleb. "Nobody *lets* me do anything."

"He just stood back while you…what, ran for your life? Is Kemp the one who's after you?"

"He didn't stand back, he…Look, I made a mistake, and I left an electronic trail when I stole that money. One of Kemp's IT people traced it back to me. What's the point in implicating Marcus when my fingerprints were all over the crime scene? Besides, it was my idea."

"And Kemp isn't smart enough to put two and two together and figure out why you stole from him?"

I shrug. "He doesn't seem to have put it together so far. I've been in touch with Marcus. I talked to him just yesterday, and he's okay."

"Does he know where you are?"

"No," I reply. "I'm not that stupid."

"If Kemp isn't after you, then who is?"

"A man named Andre Privya. Kemp hired him."

Caleb shakes his head a little, like he's trying to make sense of everything I just told him. "How do you know that?"

"I was tracking his communications."

Caleb lets out this unbelieving huff of air. "He just hired someone to kill you? Over the phone?"

"No, he never said kill. He said 'find,' although the killing might have been implied. I was surprised he was so brazen about it, but I guess when you get away with so much for so long, you feel comfortable pushing the limits."

"How much did you take?"

I swallow. I've come this far, no sense in trying to lie about it now. "Two million dollars."

Sliding his hands through his hair, Caleb bows his head, taking a deep breath.

"I didn't do it all at once, and I didn't take it all from the same account, but like I said, I made a mistake covering my tracks, and here I am."

"And your computer beeping means…what, exactly? That he found you?"

"I don't know," I say. "I had been really careful about not using my real name. I checked into the hotels under aliases, I used cash for everything. I used a burner phone to call Marcus. I didn't want to give him any way to track me, but I put an alert on my own name anyway. It pinged last night because there were pictures taken of us at the benefit, and someone gave the press my name."

Caleb starts bouncing his leg again, and then he stands, and he gives all of his pent-up rage an outlet by sliding his hand across the coffee table, and knocking everything on top of it onto the floor. "God damn it!"

I cringe at the sound of breaking glass, and look over at him.

"I'm the one who gave them your name. They asked, and I…"

"You didn't know," I say soothingly. I don't want him to have even an ounce of guilt about that. "You didn't know, Caleb."

He turns, and oh, that anger is back.

"Why didn't you tell me? I could've helped you before now. Now we're on defense, and it's better to work on offense."

I don't miss the 'we' in that sentence, but I can't let him be a part of this. I *won't*.

"I don't know what being on offense feels like anymore. And I didn't tell you, because how would that look? What would you think of me, if I had just met you and told you I had stolen money from a crooked millionaire who basically killed my father, and was responsible for ruining the life of my surrogate mother?"

Either he doesn't have an answer for me, or the only answer he can come up with isn't a good one. Not that I'd blame him one bit for running away after an admission like that. I wouldn't blame him for running away now, but it doesn't seem like he's going to do that.

"Did you think you could just stay here forever? Start a new life?"

I shrug. "I came here to get away from the situation, to give myself some time where I didn't have to look over my shoulder, and could take a breather to figure out how to make things better."

"There is no making things better when someone's sent a *hitman* after you, Mia. And you were just pretending it didn't happen?"

"No," I reply, my voice shaky. "There's no forgetting something like that, but I came here, and I met you…and you made me want something different. You…you made me hope I could have it. I didn't tell you, because I didn't want you to look at me the way you're looking at me now."

"How am I looking at you?"

"Like you don't even know me," I say, not blaming him one bit for that. "Like you're disgusted with me."

"Not for the reason that you think."

"Not because I'm a liar? Because I'm a thief?"

He glares at me. "You're neither of those things, and no, that's not it."

Caleb rubs his hand across the back of his neck, then turns and looks out the window. He's quiet for a few minutes, probably trying to figure out how he's going to end this. I decide to make it easy on him; it seems like the very least I can do.

"I'm going to go get dressed," I say, tugging on the hem of the shirt that I'm wearing. "I'll be out of here in a minute."

Caleb laughs bitterly, then turns and faces me, arms folded across his chest. "Where would you even go?"

"Back to Chicago," I tell him. "To get this over with."

"No you're not," he replies, walking toward the hallway. "You're staying right here."

"And what…you're leaving?"

"I'm going to get dressed, and then I'm going to go work out what's going on in my head. I want you here when I come back." His eyes soften then, and he looks at me tenderly. "Don't go getting any crazy ideas about turning yourself in, or leaving town. We're going to talk about this some more, I just need some time to think."

Caleb disappears down the hallway. He's gone for two minutes at the most, and walks back into the living room fully dressed. It seems like he's cooled down a little, and when he stops in front of me, he cradles my cheek with his hand. It's the most comfort I've felt all morning.

"Promise me you won't leave," he says.

"I'll be here when you get back."

He gives me a small smile, as the pad of his thumb slides across my cheekbone.

When he reaches the front door, he turns and says, "Everything's going to be okay, Mia."

I want to believe him, but this is the farthest from okay I've been in a long, long time.

CHAPTER Twenty-Four

I wait for Caleb to return to the apartment for what feels like forever. I keep a watchful eye on the clock, which just makes the time pass more slowly. He left just before noon, and the sun is beginning to set now. I don't want to panic, but I've never been out of contact with him for this long, and it's difficult not to imagine that something terrible has happened to him in the hours that he's been away.

He was in the pictures that were published of me last night. His name was in the captions, right next to mine. It'd be one thing for Privya to come after me, but if he somehow hurt Caleb…

No, I'm not going to think like that right now. My laptop is open, my tracking program is active. There haven't been any new alerts since this morning. Caleb's okay, he's just taking some time like he said he was. Nothing has happened to him.

Maybe if I want it badly enough, it'll be true.

Caleb still isn't home as the clock strikes 10, and I'm starting to get pretty desperate.

So desperate, in fact, that I've got Jack Kemp's cell phone number dialed on my phone, with my thumb hovering just above the "call" button. The waiting is killing me, and I just…I can't deal with Caleb getting involved. I don't want any issues that Kemp and Privya have with me to be taken out on Caleb.

I want this over with. Now. I always thought that I'd feel better about things once Caleb found out about what I had done, but no. It fills me with an anxiety that I can't even explain, and it makes me want him in my sight every second of every day. If I thought I was worried thinking Privya was after *me*, it's nothing compared to the possibility that he could go after Caleb.

Only the fact that I told Caleb I'd be here when he got back is keeping me in place. I'm not going to break my word.

He finally walks through the door at 10:15, and I nearly jump out of my seat. When he turns the corner into the dining room, where I'm sitting, he looks like he's been awake for days. His eyes are tired, and his hair is all disheveled, like he's been running his fingers through it all day.

"Caleb?" I want to ask him where he's been and why he looks so worn out, but I'm not sure how he'll react.

He holds out his hand. "C'mon. Let's go to bed, it's been a long day."

I look at him like he's lost his mind. "You can't come home after being gone all day, after having the conversation that we had, and just ask me to go to bed."

"Well, I just did," he says, before rubbing at his eyes.

"What did you do?"

"I didn't do anything," he replies. He so obviously doesn't want to have this conversation, but we're going to have it.

"You've been gone for over ten hours, Caleb. You did something."

He shrugs. "I was just thinking."

"About what?"

"I can't do this tonight, Mia. Okay? Let's just go to bed."

"I get that you're tired, I really do. I don't want to push you, but if you did something to try and save me, or get me out of this-"

"I was trying to figure out a way to…I don't know, to make it right."

Damn it, this is what I was worried about. It wasn't just about him knowing, it was about him wanting to get involved.

"It's not up to you to make it right," I try to explain, keeping myself as calm as I possibly can. "It's my mess, and I'm the one who has to clean it up."

Just like that, there's anger in his eyes. "How are you going to clean it up? By turning yourself in to him so he can…" He's having difficulty saying the words, but I know what's coming. "So he can kill you? No. You're not doing that."

"You said it yourself, the guy is a *hitman*!" I yell. "You don't want me involved with him any more than I want you involved with him. And if you think I'm going to let you get between me and someone who is after me for something that *I* did, you've got another thing coming."

"And if you think I'm going to let you turn yourself over because you robbed some shady slumlord who got what he deserved, then *you've* got another thing coming."

"You looked him up," I say. I can picture him at his office, sitting in front of his computer, verifying my story.

"I did," he admits.

The thought of it is comforting to me. It's what I would've done if I were in his shoes. I respect that he had doubts, that he had to verify things for himself. Maybe he just wanted to see how terrible of a person Kemp is and has been for years, and is still getting away with it.

"Good," I reply, which seems to surprise him. "So you saw everything."

"Yes. And I'm going to do something about it before something like that happens again."

I reach up and rub at my temples, trying to stave away the headache that I can feel coming on. "Like what? You can't get involved with this, Caleb."

Caleb cradles my face in his hands, but there isn't much

tenderness there, like there has been all the times before. "I love you, okay? I'm in love with you, Mia. I'm already involved."

I reach up and wrap my hands around his wrists, needing something to hold onto. He just told me he loves me, and loving me is going to wind up getting him hurt, or worse. I feel like crying, because it's everything I wanted to have, in a way that I never wanted to have it.

"I love you, too. You've done so much for me already, Caleb. I just…I did this, and I can't let you…"

Caleb leans down and presses his lips against mine. It's soft, and short, and it's nice to feel this connection with him again.

"Let's go to bed," he whispers. "We know that he knows, so that puts us in a good spot. We'll figure this out tomorrow, okay? I'm going to take care of it, and I don't want to fight anymore tonight. I'm exhausted."

I reluctantly agree, and follow behind him as he leads me into the bedroom.

When Caleb is fast asleep, breathing deep, and steady, and slow, I carefully slip out of the bed.

He told me he wanted to fix this, and there isn't a doubt in my mind that he would try. He'd probably even succeed, but at what cost? If Kemp knew what Caleb was worth, he'd want more than a repayment of the $2 million I stole from him, and

Caleb would pay it.

I can't let him do that. What if Kemp wants a stake in Caleb's business? What if he wants more than that?

No.

I'm going to put a stop to this right now.

Quietly, I get dressed in the bathroom, and grab my wallet and my phone. I won't be needing anything else for this trip.

In the kitchen, I scribble out a note to Caleb in shaky handwriting.

Caleb,

You said you wanted to help me, and I have no doubt that you'd go to great lengths to do that. If you come to my rescue with Kemp, there's no telling what he'll ask you for, and because you love me, I know you'll pay it. No matter how great the cost.

Because I love you, I'm not going to let you do that.

Thank you for everything you've done for me. Finding you was one of the great blessings of my life.

I hope I'll see you again soon.

I love you.
-Mia

I take the elevator down to the lobby, which is mostly empty. We're still in the wee hours of the morning, and the concierge and doorman aren't at their posts. They must be taking a much-needed break or something. The second I step onto the sidewalk, I start punching in the number I found for Privya. My thumb is hovering over the '9' when a large hand covers my mouth.

I feel woozy and unsteady, but strong arms are wrapped around me.

I hear the loud pops of gunfire, and then I drift away.

CHAPTER Twenty-five

I wake up in a dark, damp room. I'm tied to a chair, bound by my wrists and ankles.

Nothing is covering my mouth—I'm not gagged, like I was expecting—so whoever took me isn't worried about the possibility that I'll start screaming for help. I must be somewhere remote, or at least hidden in a place where no one's around.

I'm assuming Privya is the one who snatched me from outside of Caleb's apartment building. And the gunshots were…wait, what *were* those gunshots? Whoever it was that grabbed me wasn't the one who fired the shots, because he had one hand on my mouth, and the other arm wrapped around my middle. I guess it could've been one of Privya's goons, although…who would he have been shooting at? A wave of horror crashes over me. No, not the doorman or the concierge.

Could that be why neither one was at their post? Who else could he have shot at?

A cold trickle of realization slides down my spine, and I lean as far forward as I can, feeling like I'm going to throw up.

Caleb.

No, Caleb was sleeping when I left, it couldn't have been him. He couldn't have gotten downstairs so quickly, not without me seeing him. Unless…unless he was pretending to be asleep, but if he was, he *never* would've let me leave the apartment.

I take a deep breath to calm myself, because I just can't get worked up right now, not without having all the information. Instead, I try to come up with a plan to get out of this. Given my history, plans don't really seem to be my strong suit, and when I give an experimental tug on my bindings, I realize that a plan is entirely unnecessary. I'm bound so tight that I can barely move my hands, and it seems like I'm in the middle of the room, not against a wall or something, where I might have some hope of finding a tool that would help me cut through the ropes.

There's no getting out of this.

My arms are aching, and my neck is sore. How long have I been here? It could be hours, could be days, depending on what I was given that knocked me out.

I shake my head in the darkness. What a fool I was, thinking I could do any of this on my own terms.

A man steps out of the shadows in the corner of the room, with a sadistic grin on his face. His long, dark hair is greasy, and even from this distance, I can see the beads of sweat forming along his hairline. This man resembles the only picture I was able to find of Andre Privya, but I can't be sure it's really him.

What I can be sure of is the fact that he's pressing a bloody white towel against his upper arm, where I'm assuming he was shot.

It makes me feel better that he was the one being shot at, not the one doing the shooting. But…who was doing the shooting?

"I always enjoy the moment when a target realizes that their situation is hopeless," Privya says with a heavy accent. He's stalking toward me, his eyes narrowed, slightly unsteady on his feet. He's probably lost a ton of blood.

Good.

The first and only thing I want to ask is if Caleb is okay, but drawing attention to him is the absolute dumbest thing I could do right now. Surely Privya knows he exists, since he's obviously seen the pictures of the two of us together, and was waiting to abduct me from outside of Caleb's apartment. Still, letting Privya know that I care about Caleb would put a target on his back, provided there isn't one there already.

I got into this mess because I was trying to keep Caleb out of it. Dragging him in at this point would be moronic.

The best thing I can do is keep my mouth shut.

When Privya comes to a stop, he spits on me. Somehow, I manage not to flinch away from it, which pleases me.

"You're more goddamn trouble than you're worth," he says angrily, swiping at a trickle of blood that's rolling down his arm. He winces at the movement, and I'm glad he's in pain.

I make it a point to keep my mouth shut. He's trying to goad me into a response, and I'm not going to give him the satisfaction.

"You're smart, I'll give you that. Out of all the people I've been hired to 'locate,'" he says, actually using air quotes when he says "locate," "it took me the longest to find you." A sick grin pulls at his lips. "I knew you had gone east, but I wasn't sure where. But, everyone fucks up sometime. Lucky for me, you got pictured with your little boyfriend. My employer was beginning to question my abilities."

"Your employer is a piece of shit," I tell him. Screw not talking. If this guy is going to taunt me before he kills me, then I'm going to give it right back. "And so are you."

That comment earns me a backhand across the face, which makes sharp, intense pain bloom from my throbbing cheek. It's the same cheek the robber punched, and unfortunately for me, it still isn't healed. I do my best to hide the fact that it hurts like hell.

"He told me I could do what I want with you," he growls, sliding the tip of the gun along my jawline. I manage to maintain eye contact with him while he's taunting me, even though I'm trying to brace myself for the shot. "I'd like to just be done with you. Quick. Simple."

"If you were going to just be done with me, you would have shot me in the street."

He grins, like the thought of ending my life like that is incredibly appealing. Sick bastard.

"I was going to have a little fun at first, I admit. But the more you talk, the less inclined I am to make this easy on you."

"Can't wait," I reply sarcastically. "So, you just kill me, and that's that? He doesn't even want his money back?"

"He doesn't care about the money. He cares about power, as most men of his stature do. Nobody crosses him and gets away with it, especially not some sarcastic, thieving, lying cunt."

This time *I* spit on *him*, because *nobody* calls me that.

He laughs, and runs the backs of his fingers along the cheek he just slapped. It's almost tender, apart from the fact that he's an awful person who has been hired to, you know, kill me.

"I thought for sure that you would beg. That you would cry."

"I'm not going to beg you for anything. So whatever you're going to do, just do it."

"Ah, you won't beg me for your life, but you would beg for the life of your boyfriend."

"I don't have a boyfriend." The lie feels disgusting and

wrong coming out of my mouth, and I feel sick just saying them. But this man can't know that I care about Caleb as much as I do. He has to think that he doesn't mean anything to me. It's a difficult sell, granted, considering the fact that he found me outside of Caleb's apartment, but I have to do what I can to limit the scope of this thing.

"The pictures that I saw of you tell a different story," he says, with a sadistic amount of pleasure. "Once I'm done with you, I'll start with him."

I shake my head. "You'll never get him."

"Won't I, though? Who's to say I don't already have him?"

He's lying, he's trying to rattle me. It takes everything in me to fight off the tears. "I don't believe you."

Privya leans forward, pressing the tip of the gun against my jaw. "I'm going to take you to the point where you'll be *begging* me to kill you. And then I'm going to bring your boyfriend in here, and make you watch him die. And then we'll see if you're still running that fucking mouth of yours, huh? Maybe I'll kill you then, maybe I won't. Maybe living with what you've done and what you've seen will be enough." He presses the gun into my skin until I'm sure I'm bleeding, but the shot never comes.

At this point, I'm glad I'm tied up, because it's keeping me from shaking as badly as I probably would be if my arms were free. It's fear, anger, and adrenaline all in one, and the force of it is making my teeth chatter. I have to keep my jaw clenched to stop it.

He steps away, thankfully taking the gun along with him, and I feel like I can breathe for the first time in a while.

"Now," he says, his voice full of amusement. "Let's get started, shall we?"

He walks over to the corner, and picks up a baseball bat. He slaps his hand against it a few times, making a sickening thud. I struggle against the restraints, but it's no use. Privya walks up to me, and yanks on my hair, pulling my head back violently.

"Where should I start first? Leg?" He taps the bat against my shin. "Rib?" The body of it rolls across my side.

"Fuck you," I say, because at this point, why not?

He rears back, ready to strike what I'm sure is going to be an incredibly painful blow. I close my eyes, because I don't want to see it coming.

A gunshot surprises me, and I wince, expecting to feel the sharp pain of the shot at any moment, but it never comes.

When I open my eyes, Privya falls at my feet, eyes wide open.

Dead.

"Sam?" I ask, relieved. It's always nice to see a familiar face when a hitman was getting ready to slam you in the body with a baseball bat. Especially if that familiar face belongs to a bodyguard. I'll never fight Caleb about that again. Oh god,

Caleb.

"Hi Mia," he says, with a tight, stressed smile.

"Are you hurt? Where's Caleb? Is he okay?"

"I'm not hurt," he assures me, walking behind me so that he can undo my bindings. "Caleb's taking care of Jack Kemp."

"What do you mean he's taking care of Jack Kemp!"

"Mia," Sam says calmly. "It's going to be okay. Let me get you untied."

"How did you know where I was?"

"Mister Simmons called me and told me to be on the lookout, because he was worried you were going to do exactly what you did."

"Of course he did," I say with a sigh. "Are you the one who shot at Privya?"

He nods. "I was standing too far away. Mister Simmons wanted me to stay at street-level instead of posting a guard at your door. I was in the process of assembling a team so that we could have more coverage, but I wasn't fast enough, apparently."

"It's not your fault, Sam. I'm the idiot here."

"When the person I'm supposed to be protecting gets drugged and shoved into the back of a van, that's my fault."

"But you found me."

"Mister Simmons is the one who found out where you were, Mia. I just happened to be close enough to you to get here first. Thankfully, since I'm not entirely sure Mister Simmons knows how to shoot a gun."

Yes, that's right. Sam just shot Privya. And *killed* him. Not that I'm going to mourn his death or anything, but I am sorry that Sam had to take a life to save mine.

"I'm sorry you had to do that, Sam."

"I'm not."

He finally gets my arms undone, and I could scream from the pain once they're released. Sam runs his hands up and down my aching muscles, but it doesn't help, not really.

"Yeah, that's going to hurt for a while. Nothing I can do about that. I'm sorry."

"It's okay," I manage. "How long have I been down here, anyway?"

"The better part of a day," he replies. "How much do you remember?"

When he gets my legs undone, they don't ache anywhere near as badly as my arms do, thankfully.

I shrug. "Nothing, really. I had just woken up when you came in. Whatever he drugged me with must've been really strong."

"And I can see he got you in the cheek," Sam says, reaching out toward my face. He doesn't touch me, and I'm glad for it. I don't think I could take any more pressure on my cheek. The throbbing is out of control at this point. "Piece of shit." Sam kicks Privya's dead body, and I turn my head.

He lifts his wrist to his mouth, and mumbles something

into what looks like a watch.

"What's going to happen here?" I ask.

"We're going to take care of it." Sam turns his head, and waves in two gentlemen wearing dark suits.

Sam helps me up, wrapping his arm around me to keep me steady, as he gives instructions to two guys who must be members of his security team.

"Come on," he says, leading me toward the door. "Mister Simmons is anxious to see you."

Sam leads me outside into the blazingly bright sun. I've been in that dark room for so long that it actually hurts to open my eyes. I hold my hand up against my forehead, trying to block out the never-ending brightness, and squint. I look around, and…god, Privya took me way out of the city. We're standing in front of what looks like an abandoned strip mall. It's so old that all the store windows have been busted out, and there's broken plaster everywhere.

I want to take ten showers to wash this entire experience off of me.

At the far edge of the parking lot, an SUV takes the corner without slowing down, wheels screeching against the hot asphalt. It's kicking up dust and dirt in its wake, and it makes its way along the side walk, the back door opening before it even comes to a stop.

Caleb covers the space between us in two long strides, and gathers me up in his arms, crushing me against his chest.

"What the hell were you thinking?" he asks loudly, breathlessly. He sounds like he's on the verge of completely losing it, like he's hanging on by the thinnest string.

The adrenaline I was feeling earlier is gone, and exhaustion along with the full weight of what just happened to me hits all at the same time. All I can do is cling to Caleb, and finally let all the tears and the fear that I had been holding in just…come out. I'm crying almost hysterically, my breath hitching in my chest, and the more I try to calm down, the worse it gets.

When I finally get to the point where I can manage to speak, I say, "I didn't want him to hurt you, that's all I was thinking. I didn't want you to get involved, and I didn't want to lose you."

"And how do you think I would've dealt with losing you like that? What do you think that would've done to me?"

"I'm sorry," I reply. "I'm so sorry."

He tilts my head up, and kisses me. There's a desperate, needy edge to it that surprises me, because we're not alone. Usually, in front of other people, Caleb keeps it chaste.

Not today. Not after everything that's happened.

When he finally pulls away, he runs his hands up and down my arms. He takes a step back and gives me a once-over, maintaining contact all the while. It's like he's scared to let go, like if he lets go, he thinks I'll disappear again.

"Shit," he says, gently skimming the backs of his fingers along my aching cheek. It's swollen again, I know it. I can feel my heartbeat pounding beneath the skin there. "Are you okay? We need to get you to a doctor."

"Can we just…" I take my hand and place it over his. "Can we not right now?"

Caleb wraps me in his arms again, and rocks me a little. His lips press against the crown of my head. "Sure," he replies. "I understand. I just want you to know that no one can hurt you, okay? Not now, not ever."

I lift my head back, and look into his eyes. "What did you do?"

"I got involved," he replies, and he's almost defiant about it. "And I'm still here."

There's a commotion behind me, with Sam and some other guys. Caleb turns my head against his chest, and I wonder if Privya's dead body is back there somewhere. Trying to preoccupy myself, I catch sight of Caleb's busted-up knuckles and bruised hand.

"What happened?" I ask.

"Come on," he says, leading me toward the SUV. "We can talk about it at home."

Home.

That sounds really good right about now, and I'm beginning to realize that it means something different to me now than it used to.

In the warmth of Caleb's apartment, he and I are cuddled up together on the couch. I'm in a pair of yoga pants and a t-shirt, my hair still damp from the long shower that we shared not too long ago. Caleb took his time washing my hair, and washing my body, making me feel treasured, and loved, and safe. Two half-empty cups of hot chocolate are sitting on the coffee table. Caleb made a batch after I made an offhanded comment that my mother used to make it for me when I wasn't feeling well as a child.

My arms are wrapped around Caleb's middle, my ear pressed against his chest, where I can feel the steady thrumming of his heartbeat. He's holding a bag of ice against my cheek, and I'm holding one across his swollen, busted-up knuckles.

"I'm so angry with you, I almost can't see straight," he says, pulling me closer to him, as he plants a kiss on the top of my head. "That you would take off after I explicitly asked you not to-"

"Caleb," I say sharply. I push myself up, ready to argue with him, because haven't we already had this conversation once? The one where I let him know that he doesn't get to tell me what to do?

"It's not about me telling you what to do, Mia. It's about the two of us being a team, figuring things out together. I know you were scared, but-"

"I was worried that if Kemp or Privya knew how much you meant to me, that one or both of them would use you to get to me. I didn't want you getting wrapped up in it, or doing something stupid to get me out of that mess."

"I'm going to ignore the fact that you think I'm stupid," he says, but there's a teasing undertone to it that makes me smile.

"I don't think you're stupid, but as I think I've demonstrated fairly well today, love can make you do really stupid things. And I knew that once Kemp looked into you, that he'd go after your wealth, or your company in order to get you to make a deal to get me off the hook. He's just that kind of sleaze bag."

"Yes," Caleb says, sighing. "He's exactly that kind of sleaze bag."

Oh no. *No*. "Caleb," I sigh. "You can't."

I look up at him, and he's actually giving me a cocky little grin.

"Lucky for you, I'm an amazing negotiator. And I don't go into negotiations unprepared."

"That's what you did while you were out?" While I was sitting here, nervously following my tracking program, Caleb was one step ahead of me.

"Yes," he says.

"What did you have to give him?"

"It's not important."

I sigh, and fight back the anger that's rising up inside of me. "It's important to me."

"I'm being literal here," he replies patiently. "What I had to give him isn't important. Not in the grand scheme of things."

"Oh god." All I can think about is that he's given up shares in his company, or something huge that's going to come back to bite him later.

"Mia," Caleb whispers, tilting my head up. "I know what you're thinking, and I'm telling you…it's nothing that's more important to me than you are. Besides, I told you. I'm an excellent negotiator."

"It's just…it's a lot. For me, a person who came into your life and brought trouble right along with me."

"No," he says with a smile. "Brought happiness along with you."

A wave of unexpected warmth floods my body, and I press a soft kiss against Caleb's lips. "You make me happy, too."

"What I need you to understand is that I didn't do what I did out of some kind of overbearing need to protect you."

I raise my brow, and he gives me a sheepish look.

"Okay," he replies, smiling. "It's not *just* about that."

"What's it about then?"

"I want you to be happy. You'd never be happy if you were running from somebody."

That answer earns him another kiss. This one, it lingers.

"And you're really not going to tell me what you agreed to?"

He shakes his head. "I didn't agree to anything, really.

Turns out, I know quite a few people who have done business with Jack Kemp, and he's screwed over more than a couple of them. Not to sound like an asshole, but I'm five times the businessman he is, and ten times as rich. All the shit he pulled on those poor, unsuspecting people who couldn't stand up to him? That doesn't work on me. "

He does sound like an asshole, but in a ridiculously hot kind of way. I decide not to tell him that, just to make my life easier in the future.

Caleb's eyebrows scrunch together before he starts talking again, and his eyes get this distant, faraway look in them. "Getting him to tell me where you were, that was the most difficult part. I did have to…make some concessions to get that information, and I was more than willing to do that." He looks down at me tenderly, and cups my cheek. "I've never been so scared in my life."

I turn my head, and kiss the palm of his hand. "I'm sorry I scared you. I did it for what I thought was a really good reason at the time."

"I know you did," he says, nodding. He looks more like himself now. "I'm going to be mad at you about it for a really long time, though."

"I know," I admit quietly. "Does it mean anything if I tell you it won't happen again?"

He nods. "It helps. It would mean more to me if you promised me that in the future, if you're ever in any kind of trouble where you even consider doing something like you did with Kemp, that you'll come to me before you do anything..."

Caleb hesitates before he finishes that sentence. "It's okay, you can say stupid."

"Okay," he laughs. "Come to me before you do anything stupid. I know this thing between us is still new, and I don't know where it's going to go, especially now that you can safely go back to Chicago, just...come to me first. Please."

To be honest, I hadn't even considered the thought that I *could* go back to Chicago. I'm guessing it means something that the thought didn't even enter my mind until just now, when Caleb brought it up.

"I can't imagine another situation where I'll need to steal from a sleazy slumlord to pay someone's medical bills," I reply, trying to lighten the mood.

With Caleb the way he is right now, laser-focused on the task at hand, there is no lightening this mood. "Promise me."

"I promise."

Caleb lets out a sigh of relief, and gives me a squeeze.

"May I ask what you got Kemp to agree to?"

"Forgiveness of the two million," Caleb replies. "We both agreed that he owed you that and more for pain and suffering, so he wrote me a check, which I'll give to you later."

"I don't want his money," I tell him. Maybe that's foolish of me, but I really, really don't.

Caleb squeezes my shoulder. "I didn't say you had to keep it."

I grin. "Fair enough."

"He's going to continue paying for your friend's mother to get treatment for her burns. And he's going to get all the other buildings that he owns up to code, so this doesn't happen again. I got him to sign a contract to that effect, so there's no backing out of it now."

I'm struck by a swooping sensation in my stomach at Caleb's confession, and I have to blink back the tears that are stinging my eyes. The fact that Caleb not only went to bat for me, to get me out of the ridiculous mess that I got myself into in the first place, but that he went above and beyond to make sure that Amelia was taken care of, and stopped Kemp from being able to let this happen to another person? It makes me fall in love with him a little more.

Okay…a *lot* more.

"Thank you," I whisper, bringing his injured hand to my lips. When I look into his eyes, I know he can see what I'm struggling to find the words to tell him. There's no way I could ever sufficiently express what this means to me.

"I would do anything for you," he says, smiling.

"Even beat the shit out of Jack Kemp? Which I'm assuming you did, based on the state of your hand?"

"You are assuming correctly. And I would've killed Privya, if I had gotten there in time."

"I'm glad you didn't," I admit. "Not that I like the fact that Sam *did*, but I don't want blood on your hands. Not because of me. Is Sam going to…I mean, what happens now?" I can't bring myself to ask what happens to the body. I'm guessing they're not going to report it to the police, and it's going to be like Privya never existed. It's also probably smart if Caleb doesn't answer that question.

"Don't worry about that," Caleb says, with a finality that I know not to argue with.

I nod, then tilt my head up to kiss him.

He brings his forehead to rest against mine, and whispers, "There were a few minutes this afternoon when I was worried I wasn't going to get to see you again." He pulls me on top of him, until I'm straddling his thighs. I kiss him again, but this time it's long, and slow, and deep.

"I'm here," I tell him. "I'm right here." Gingerly, I bring his hand up to my chest, resting his palm right over my heartbeat. "Do you feel that? It's still beating because of you."

He lets his hand rest between the valley of my breasts for a moment, and then I lift my shirt up and off, tossing it on the floor behind me. Caleb's breath catches.

"Take off your shirt," I say, and he complies immediately. "I want to show you how good it feels to be alive."

I sit up on my knees, bringing myself closer to Caleb's height. He slides his arms around my waist, and pulls me close, kissing his way across my collarbone. My hands roam across every inch of skin they can reach: across his pecs, down his abs, and finally they tease along the waistband of his pants. I rock against him steadily, feeling him get harder and harder between my legs. I love the soft noises that find their way out of Caleb's mouth as I move. He breathes them into me, kissing my lips hungrily. I dip my hand down under his sweatpants, brushing my thumb across the bead of moisture at the head of Caleb's cock.

His hips thrust up into my touch, in a slow, steady rhythm. Tonight, though, I don't want to tease him. I don't want to draw this out, and I certainly don't want to wait. I just want him. *Now.*

Caleb groans when I ease myself up, but his eyes hungrily follow my movement as I push my pants down to the floor. "Take them off," I say, letting him know that I want him to do the same.

A slow, sexy grin spreads across his face as he lifts his hips and slides his pants down. He kicks them off to the side, then pulls me back down on top of him. I move my hips, sliding against his hard length, as he takes one of my nipples into his mouth. On a downward pass, I shift at just the right angle, and he slides inside of me.

We both exhale at the unexpected pleasure, and Caleb cups my face, pulling me close. My top lip is brushing his, but we're not kissing. We're just looking at each other with heavy lidded eyes, our breaths rough and ragged. Caleb traces the pad of his thumb along the curve of my lower lip, admiring my features like he's trying to memorize everything.

"Don't scare me like that again, okay? I…I don't think I

could take it."

The unexpected heaviness and meaning in his voice takes me by surprise, and I wrap my arms around him. His head rests in the crook of my neck, his fingers digging into the skin on my back.

"I won't," I promise, and Caleb nods, closing his eyes.

Our bodies rock together, slow and unhurried. Tonight it's more about the act of being close, of loving and being loved, than chasing any kind of pleasure (although there's pleasure - lots of it). It's long sighs and soft kisses. It's whispered words of love and comfort.

We come together, riding out the steady, strong waves that feel amazing, and are both emotionally and physically intense. Caleb and I have always been somewhat desperate to find release, but tonight we're just desperate to get lost in each other. Again, and again, and again.

After, Caleb curls around me on the couch, our arms and legs twined together. It's comforting and safe, and I kind of want to stay here for the rest of my life. I could do that, easily, but I've got some unfinished business out there in the world, and I'm ready to take care of it.

"Caleb," I whisper. He's breathing so deeply that I'm not sure he's still awake.

"Yeah," he replies sleepily.

I take a deep breath, and swallow. "I want to go back to Chicago."

CHAPTER Twenty-Seven

Standing in the foyer of my apartment in Chicago, I feel this odd sense of relief wash over me. If I'm completely honest with myself, when I was packing my things into the bag that I took with me to New York, I didn't really think I'd ever come back here. I thought Privya would kill me, or—best case scenario—I would be on the run for the rest of my life.

I never could've imagined that I'd meet and fall in love with a wonderful man who would change my life in so many ways, and give me a future I didn't think I would have the last time I was in this apartment. So, I'm glad he's here with me now, standing by my side as I take some time to decide what exactly I'm going to *do* with that future.

The first thing we did upon arrival was make a stop at my mailbox, where over a month's worth of junk was piled up inside. Caleb's holding it all in the crook of his right arm, and our bags are slung over his left.

"You can put that over there on the table," I tell him, pointing to my left. "Sorry, it's…it's kind of sparse in here." I take a step into the living area, which is the complete opposite the lush apartment that Caleb has in New York. This whole place is about half the size of his bedroom, and that's being generous.

I lost almost everything I owned in the explosion, and I rented this studio a week after, when I was tired of sleeping on Marcus's couch. I was living my life in a daze back then, still grieving, still unbelieving. I never bothered to put up any pictures on the wall, and barely even decorated the place. I didn't ever think of it as "home" so much as a temporary resting place. Seems like that's exactly what it turned out to be.

All I have in here is a bed, a comfy chair I picked up at a thrift store, and an old bookshelf filled with my favorite books that I had replaced at a secondhand bookstore. I walk over to the window, and slide my fingertips across the arms of that old chair. I spent a lot of time curled up in this thing. Sometimes I was hard at work, laptop balanced precariously on my lap. Sometimes I was reading, curled up with a blanket and a good book, hoping I could forget about life for a while. Sometimes I just sat down and cried.

The air is a little stuffy, because the place doesn't have central air, and the windows have been shut ever since I left. There's just a musty, un-lived in smell, and I'm grateful that I had the presence of mind to throw away all of my food before I left. Otherwise, this place would be unbearable.

I turn to Caleb, who's standing next to my bed. He's looking around with this small smile on his face, like he knows something that I don't.

"What?" I ask, amused. "What's that look for?"

Caleb shrugs, and takes a step toward me. "This place is very you."

"It's not even decorated, Caleb. Anyone could live here."

"No, not anyone. This," he says, bending down and sliding his fingers across the blanket at the end of my bed. "You wear this color a lot. And your pillows..." He points out the way they're tossed on the bed, two to rest my head on and one behind me. "You sleep like that, even with me." He lifts up one of the pillows, and smiles when he finds a pair of pajamas folded underneath. "You do this at home, too."

I don't miss his mention of "home," like it's there in New York, not here in this tiny apartment hundreds of miles away from the life that we're building together.

"Those are books that you want to read, but haven't gotten to yet," he says, pointing at the small stack next to the chair. "Just like you have at home. There are a couple of the same books here."

The look on my face must convey what I'm feeling at the moment: complete shock. "You notice all of that?"

Caleb closes the distance between us, then leans down and

gives me a kiss. "I notice a lot of things about you."

I caress his cheek. "Why don't you have a seat? I should go through all of this mail."

Caleb nods, then lowers himself onto my chair. He leans forward, and starts thumbing through the books on my shelf. I'm struck by the sight of him here, surprised that he doesn't seem out of place at all. I mean, there's something about Caleb that exudes wealth, and he still looks right sitting on my second hand chair, looking through my secondhand books. I fit right into his world, too.

Something about that realization strikes me hard in the chest.

"Mia?"

"Yeah?"

"C'mere," he says softly. When he asks like that, I can't help but comply.

I walk over, and sit down on his lap, then swing my legs over the arms of the chair. Caleb wraps his arm around my back, and places a hand on my knee, rubbing small circles across the skin there with his thumb.

"Tell me what you're thinking?" he asks, before pressing a kiss to my temple.

I take a deep breath, then tell him, "I'm thinking that this is a little surreal."

"How so?"

"I…I'm just not sure how I ended up here. It seems a little

too good to be true."

"Well," he replies with a teasing lilt in his voice. "We got on a plane and flew."

I reach up and scrub my hand across his stubbly cheek, and laugh. This man, he makes me happy. Happier than I've been in my entire life, actually. He lit the spark inside of me that seemed to burn out after my father died.

"When I left here, I thought I wouldn't ever come back. Well…not under any good circumstances, at least. I didn't think I'd see this place again, and when I met you, I just…I kept waiting for the other shoe to drop. I was sure that when you found out about what I'd done you wouldn't want anything to do with me. You've been so wonderful and supportive, and it's more than I ever could've dared to hope for. And now, I have the choice between two lives. I never thought…" I trail off at the end, because I'm afraid I'm going to start crying. This is a happy sentiment; I don't want to ruin it with tears.

"I'm not going to pressure you, Mia. I told you we could make this work."

"I know," I say softly. "I just never thought I'd get to this point, you know? Where I was safe here, where you were here with me."

"I want to be wherever you are," he replies, kissing the underside of my jaw. "Wherever that is."

I run my fingers through his thick hair, loving Caleb's hum of satisfaction. "You're being so supportive, but I know you must have an opinion."

He presses his lips together, then looks down at the floor. "I do, of course I do. But I don't want to give it to you."

"What if I asked you for it?"

I see just the hint of a smile, before Caleb answers. "I still don't want to give it to you."

"You know that makes me want it even more, right?"

"So," he replies, twining our fingers together. "Say I give this opinion to you. What happens in the future if things don't work out the way you hoped or expected them to, and you resent me because you feel like my opinion swayed you one way or the other?"

"Caleb," I sigh. "I could never resent you."

"You know who has said that before?"

"Who?"

"A person who resents another person." He brings my hand up to his lips, and gives me a kiss. But he's grinning at me, and that's a good sign. "I want you to come back to New York, Mia. I want you to live with me, and I want us to have a home and a life together, and that's what I can promise you right now. But that's what *I* want. If that's not what you want…I realize this involves uprooting your life."

"I already uprooted my life." The fact is, I've already moved to New York, I've already changed everything. I just have the option of undoing that now if I want to.

"That was because you didn't have a choice. If you're going

to do it this time, willingly, I want you to do it because that's what *you* want to do, not because it's what I want you to do."

"Thank you for that. And thank you for telling me."

Caleb leans in and kisses me. "Thank you for asking my opinion."

"Do you want to stay here tonight?" I ask. "Or we could find a hotel, if you want to."

"I want to stay here tonight."

That's the answer I was hoping to get, so I can't help but beam at him. "Good."

"What are your plans for the rest of the day?"

"I'd like to go see Marcus and Amelia," I tell him.

"I think that's a great idea."

"Would you like to come with me?" I ask hopefully.

I can tell from the look on his face that he's struggling with an answer. At least, struggling to figure out a way to tell me his answer.

"I think you should spend some time with your friend and his mother. I don't want you to feel like you have to invite me because of everything that happened. I think I'd probably be a third wheel."

Sliding my fingertip along the placket of Caleb's shirt, I say, "Marcus is going to want to thank you, you know. I told him about everything you did for us. He hates Jack Kemp as much as I do."

The corner of Caleb's mouth quirks up. "I like him already."

“You’re going to like him a lot,” I promise.

“You go alone. How about we have a late lunch with Marcus?”

I nod, smiling. “Yeah. I’d like that.”

CHAPTER Twenty-Eight

I didn't cry when Caleb and I walked down my street, and I didn't cry when we walked into my apartment, but when Marcus wraps his arms around me for the first time in what feels like forever, that's when the tears finally break free. He holds on tight, like he has since we were younger, and whatever awkwardness there is between us for what I've done for him and his mother, it's gone for the time being. It's just the two of us, without the weight of responsibility between us.

"I'm so glad you're back," he says, as I reach up to wipe a tear from his cheek. "I've missed you."

"I'm glad I'm back, too. I didn't think…I didn't think I'd ever be able to show my face here again." I didn't think I'd ever talk to Marcus on anything other than an untraceable cell phone again, either.

"So…that's it?" he asks, leading me to a quiet corner at

the end of the hallway in his mother's care facility. "It's all over now?"

I told him the details of the deal Caleb made with Jack Kemp over the phone, but it's still hard to believe. I understand why he wants me to say the words again. He'll probably ask me again at some point; I know I had to ask Caleb more than once if it was true.

"It's over. Your mom's going to be taken care of, and this isn't going to happen again. Not to anyone who lives in any of his other buildings."

Marcus grins as he lets out a breath of relief. "I'm going to need you to tell me that again sometime."

I laugh. "I know."

"I've got to meet the guy who pulled this one off. Is he here?"

"No," I reply, shaking my head. "I think he wanted us to have some time just the two of us. I think there's another part of him that's just really modest, and was worried about what it might look like if he showed up here. I think he didn't want you to feel like you owe him anything."

"Mia," Marcus says incredulously. "I owe him everything."

"He's weird like that," I reply with a wide smile."

Marcus's eyes widen, and he smiles. He looks lighter, happier than I've seen him in a long time. I've almost forgotten what he looks like when he's happy. "You're in love with him."

"Yeah, I am." I'm not even going to try to deny it.

"Who would've thought? When you took off that night, who would've thought this could happen?"

"Not me, that's for sure," I say, laughing.

Marcus wraps his arms around me, giving me another long, tight hug. "I can never thank you enough for what you did for us."

Even though it was one of the stupidest things I've ever done, I can't find it in myself to regret it. It led me here, to this point. "How is she doing?" I ask, motioning toward the door that leads to Amelia's room.

"She's doing okay. She had another operation yesterday, and her doctors have her in a medically induced coma. She's probably not going to be awake for a while."

I ask the question that I've been avoiding for a while, but I just have to know. "Is she ever going to get out of here?" This is a really nice facility, but I can't imagine spending an extended period of time in a hospital, no matter how nice it is. Knowing Amelia—as independent as she was—she wouldn't want that, either. She's always been so bright and full of life, and all I want is for her to get back to that point, or as close as she can get to it.

Marcus looks down at the floor, where he shuffles his feet. "It's going to be a while, but the doctors are hopeful. The only reason she's gotten as far as she has is because of you, and I..." He bows his head as he trails off. I step up, and hug him.

"I know," I say soothingly. "I know."

"You want to go see her?"

I nod. "Yeah."

We walk into the room, and I'm struck by the sight of Amelia, laying still in her bed, wrapped from head to toe in bandages. She's attached to so many tubes and machines, and all I can hear in the room is the steady beeping of her heart monitor, and the gentle whoosh of the machine that's breathing for her.

I have to swallow down the lump that's rising in my throat. I can't cry, not now. How many times has she held it together while sitting by my bedside, trying to make me feel better? Even if she can't hear me, I have to be here for her now. So, I do what she always did for me. I pull a chair up to the side of her bed, and gently wrap my hand around the tips of her fingers, which are bandage-free.

Then I lean forward, and start humming.

CHAPTER Twenty-Nine

Later, after the hospital nurses kick Marcus and me out of the room so that Amelia can get some rest, we meet Caleb at our favorite pizza place. Like I expected, Caleb and Marcus hit it off instantly. We're sitting in the corner of the restaurant, and Caleb is nursing a beer while Marcus regales him with tales of my most embarrassing moments.

"She what?" Caleb asks, laughing so hard that he's almost doubled over.

"She shoved it right up her nose," Marcus replies. "And it fit! Her nostrils are huge."

"What?!" I cry, completely offended. "They are not! And it was one of the plain candies, not the kind with peanuts in it. It's not like it took a lot of work to get it up there." God, why am I helping them with this? "I was a curious kid, okay?"

If anything, Caleb looks at me like these stupid,

embarrassing stories have made him fall even more in love with me. I'm glad that it's going to end whenever we leave, it's not like I'm going to reveal any of these things about myself. This must be what it feels like to have your mother sit down with your boyfriend and show him your baby photos. I suppose if there's a positive to having all of my embarrassing baby pictures incinerated in an explosion, it's that they can't ever be used as ammunition for embarrassment.

Laughing, Caleb leans forward and kisses me. "I love you," he says. "But I guess I'm going to have to watch you around the bite-sized candy from now on." I give him a light smack on the wrist, and glare at Marcus, who's cackling.

When the laughter dies down, Marcus turns to Caleb. "I can't thank you enough for what you did for my mother and me, what you did for Mia, and what you did for all the other tenants in Kemp's buildings who don't have any way out of that situation. None of them know that you probably just saved their lives."

Caleb gives him a warm smile, and simply says, "You're welcome." No long speeches, or heartfelt anecdotes. "I hope your mother gets better, and I hope that you'll keep me updated." He reaches into his pocket, pulls out a business card, and hands it to Marcus. "If you need anything, my number's on there. Or, you can let Mia know. I'll make sure that it gets taken care of."

Marcus is visibly touched, and he's fighting through the

emotions he's feeling. He and I aren't the kind of people who have ever had someone go out of their way to care for us. It's a difficult thing to accept, and it's hard to do gracefully sometimes.

"I will do that," Marcus finally replies, his voice wavering. "Thank you so much." I see Marcus's gaze move to where Caleb is holding my hand on the table, and he gives me a smile.

Caleb's phone rings, and he quickly pulls it out of his pocket, his eyes narrowing when he looks at the screen. "This is rude, I apologize, but I need to take this call."

Marcus nods. Caleb kisses my cheek, then squeezes my hand as he leaves.

"You're going back to New York with him," Marcus says. There isn't any sadness in his voice, just…happiness. For me.

"I haven't decided yet," I reply, twisting my fingers together.

"Yes you have. Do I really need to say it?"

"Say what?" I ask.

"This isn't where you belong anymore."

After Caleb and I leave the pizza place, we take a tour of *my* Chicago. We walk past my high school, the playground where I broke my leg jumping off of the swing set when I was 12. We get a cupcake at my favorite bakery, and dip our feet into my favorite fountain. As we walk around, I realize that despite how much I love this city, and the fact that it holds countless dear memories for me, it doesn't feel like *home*. Not anymore.

We meet a few of my friends for drinks at bar I worked at during summer break before my last year of college, and Caleb charms them all. I haven't told anyone that I'm leaving for good, but all of them seem to know that I'm not coming back. They say their goodbyes, one by one, as they clear out of the bar.

Later, when Caleb and I are lying naked on my sheets, a cool, gentle breeze blows through the open windows. My bed is nowhere near as comfortable as Caleb's is. It's a little too small, and the sheets are a little too scratchy, but being in it with Caleb feels right.

I'm lying on my stomach, my head resting on a pillow, facing Caleb.

Caleb's on his side, watching me, sliding his fingertips up and down my spine. Each pass makes me shiver, and Caleb grins every time I do it.

"I like Marcus," he says. "I can see why you were willing to do what you did for him and his mother."

"I love him," I reply. "Things are a little weird between us now. Not all the way off, but not the way that they were before. I crossed a line for him, and now things are strained, and I'm not sure if they'll ever be the same again. I mean, it's not like we can't be friends anymore, nothing like that. Just…different, I suppose. Like a piece in the puzzle popped out a little, and neither one of us can put it back. Does that make sense?"

Caleb leans down and kisses my shoulder. "It makes sense to me. You went above and beyond, and he feels like there isn't any way for him to make it up to you."

"Maybe," I say, giving that some thought. He doesn't need to make it up to me at all. "I think he feels like what I did for him changed my life. But after meeting you, I think he realizes that it's a good thing."

"Is it?"

"Yeah. It made me realize that this?" I say, waving my hand in the air. "It's my house, but it's not my home."

He smiles, knowing exactly what I'm getting at, but needing to hear it just the same. "What are you saying?"

"You know what I'm saying," I tease. "What you said earlier about building a home with you, it sounded really good, but-"

"But?" His eyebrows practically raise up to his hairline.

"But I think I've already done it."

Caleb's lips slowly stretch up into a smile, until he's beaming. That smile is bright as the sun, even here in this dark room.

"So what does that mean?" he asks.

"Well, I was thinking that after I complete the work I'm doing for my current clients, I could go talk to Ben." I roll over onto my side, and thread my fingers through Caleb's. "Maybe his offer will still stand after he takes a look at my work."

"And you'll stay with me?" God, the look on his face takes my breath away. I want to put that look on his face every day for the rest of my life.

"As long as you'll have me."

Caleb rolls over on top of me, his body pressed against mine. The weight of him feels amazing, and familiar. He anchors himself on his left arm, as he leans down and kisses me. "I'll have you," he whispers against my lips.

"I love you," I tell him.

"I love you," he replies.

"Tomorrow, after one last bagel from my favorite shop, let's go home."

CHAPTER *Thirty*

The offices of Williams Software are about what I expected for a cutting-edge software developer. Most leaders in this industry are big on keeping the creative juices flowing, and want coders who spend long days in front of a computer to have a place where they can go and blow off some steam. There are games everywhere, bright paintings and photos on the walls, and the typical cubicle farm was done away with in favor of open workspaces. People are dressed casually, but they aren't sloppy, and the second I step through the front doors, I feel welcome.

Ben's office is a little more subdued than the rest of the workspace, looking a lot like what you'd expect a CEO's office to look like, with the exception of his wall decor. Instead of hanging up high-end art, Ben has opted to display prototype gaming systems covered with plexiglass. It's a fun space, but you get the definite impression that this is a place where the boss works.

From what he's told me about the company so far, it seems as if Ben likes to foster a pleasant work environment, and isn't set on having his employees follow a rigid schedule from nine to five. People here are encouraged to collaborate and nurture each other's ideas. If I'm going to leave the world of consulting, this is the type of company that I want to work at.

It's funny, when I walked into this building for my interview today, I wouldn't have been heartbroken if I didn't get this job. After seeing the space, and meeting some of the employees, I definitely want this job. Wanting it as badly as I do is what is making the pace at which Ben is reviewing my work even more maddening. He's scrolling through the screens, clicking, and making faces that I don't know him well enough to decipher. I think they're good, but I have no idea. He asks me questions occasionally, like why I omitted a feature, or what made me choose to code something a particular way. Apart from that, he's mostly silent, engrossed in his work.

"I'm really impressed with you, Mia," he finally says, and relief washes over me. "You developed all of this software on your own?"

"Yes," I say, nodding. "That's all work that I did on my own."

"Wow. Some of this is incredibly advanced work. You do have some areas where you can improve."

I'm still young, still fresh out of college, so I'm not surprised to hear him say this. I definitely have my weaknesses. I won't lie and say it doesn't sting a little to hear the words out loud, though. I appreciate that Ben is willing to be honest with me, and that he's not pulling any punches because we know each other personally.

"As you know," he says, leaning his elbows on his desk, "Williams is a leader in the industry, and we've got several large projects in development. I've got teams in place for all but one, and that's what I'd like your help with."

"Okay," I reply, anxious to hear about this project. I know before he starts talking that I'm going to want to work on it. I want to learn anything I can from the developers that he's hired to work here.

He describes the challenges that they're running into with this particular client, and his needs fit well with some of my skill areas. I'd also be working with some engineers who can help fill in the gaps in my knowledge base.

"I'm a firm believer in working your way up, Mia," he explains. "But this work you've been doing on your own is well above entry level. I don't think you're ready to lead your own team yet, but I don't want you to waste away on the bottom rung of the ladder. I'd like you to work on the development team; I think that's where you'd learn the most, and be the biggest asset to the company and the project."

"Okay," I reply, trying not to sound as excited as I feel.

"And this is purely based on my work and my potential, not the fact that I'm dating your best friend?"

Ben grins at me. "Oh, it's definitely based on the content of your work. The fact that you're dating my best friend actually lowers my opinion of your decision-making skills," he replies with a playful wink.

I can't help but laugh.

"So," he says, reaching into his desk and pulling out a sticky note. He uncaps a pen and starts writing. "I'm going to have HR put together a formal offer package for you. Read it over, and decide if the offer is fair and acceptable. I have a preliminary offer as far as salary goes." He holds out the sticky note, so I can see what's written on it.

Wow. Like...*wow*. It takes every bit of control I have to make sure my eyes don't get comically large and pop out of my head looking at this number. There are six figures here. I mean, not a crazy large kind of six figures, but...six figures.

"Yes," I reply, my voice cracking. "I think that's fair."

"Good." He takes the note and sticks it on the folder that he inserted my resume into earlier. "I'm glad everything worked out."

Ben gives me this look, this loaded *look*, and I realize that he's trying to let me know that he knows about what went on between me and Jack Kemp, and possibly the whole Privya situation. I appreciate the gesture, because I wouldn't want to worry about that coming to light every day, wondering whether I was on the verge of getting fired or not.

"I'm glad, too."

"I'll get that offer letter out to you as soon as I can, okay? Tomorrow, probably. Then we can discuss your start date."

"Sounds good," I tell him.

Ben stands up, and I follow suit. He reaches across his desk, and shakes my hand. He walks me through the office, and out into the elevator lobby.

"Do I need to bring anything to the cookout on Sunday?" he asks.

"Nope, just yourself. And maybe some backup steaks, because Caleb insists on grilling."

Ben laughs. "That's a recipe for disaster. You got it."

"I'll see you at seven?"

"Seven sounds great."

CHAPTER Thirty-One

"Why are you hovering?" Caleb asks. I can't tell if he's *really* irritated, or if he's *pretending* to be irritated.

"There are a few reasons," I reply.

"How about if you tell me what they are?"

"Okay, well, first of all, I like watching. I have a nice view from over here." I'm not even kidding about this view, which is, quite frankly, amazing. Caleb is wearing the perfect pair of jeans today, they make his ass look perfect. I'm not about to say that in front of his friends, though, who are sitting a few feet behind us.

Caleb looks over at me, giving me a wink and a smile.

"Those jeans are great, is all I'm saying. Buy more of them," I say. There are general sounds of mumbling coming from the peanut gallery over there, but I ignore them. "The second reason is because I continue to be fascinated by the fact that we're having a cookout on the fiftieth floor. That's backyard territory back where I'm from. Since this is a new experience, I want to be close to the action." Yes, we are fifty floors up, but this terrace is pretty amazing. Caleb had a decorator set up a little living space, so there's a couch, a love seat, and some tables in the far corner. There's even a rug in the center of the arrangement, like it's an actual living room. It still boggles my mind.

"What's the third reason?"

"Given your unfortunate history with accidentally setting things on fire, I feel better keeping an eye on things. If there's a fire up here, we're in real trouble."

Caleb rolls his eyes. "I'm not going to set anything on fire."

"I bet you said that the other times you set things on fire, huh?" I make it a point to sound like I'm teasing him, but he probably did say that those other times. I know him well enough to be able to assume it happened.

"Technically, it's already on fire. Being a grill and all," Oliver says.

"Smartass," Caleb and I say at the same time. We grin at each other like a couple of lovesick idiots.

"Let's not tempt fate, Oliver," I reprimand.

"Don't you have something you should be doing in the kitchen?" Caleb asks.

I can hear the sharp intakes of breath from Ben and Oliver, because even they know that Caleb has messed up.

I furrow my brow. “Did you just tell me to get back in the kitchen?” I’m not upset or anything, but Caleb doesn’t need to know that. I can get more mileage out of this teasing if he thinks that I am.

“I…uh…” he stutters, his eyes a little panicked. It’s pretty cute, so I let him go on like that for a few more seconds. “I didn’t mean it like that. I just know that you’re making some things, so I wondered if you, um…needed to get back to that.”

“Relax,” I say, walking up behind him and resting my head on his shoulder. “I know you’d never tell the little woman to get back in the kitchen. Besides, I’m all done. We’re just waiting on you to finish the meat. I think I have something that might speed it up.”

“Oh yeah? What’s that?”

“I can’t wait to see this,” Ben says, taking a sip of his beer.

“If history dictates,” Oliver replies dryly, “you probably don’t want to see it.”

“Hey!” I try to act offended, but they did walk in on something earlier, when Caleb and I lost track of time. Nothing indecent, just…borderline. “I made most of your food, and you don’t want to mess with the person who makes the food. Unless that person is Caleb, because messing with Caleb is fun.”

“I heard that,” Caleb shouts from his spot in front of the grill.

“I meant you to!” I slide the patio door open, and grab the

surprise for Caleb that I stashed on the table. I walk up behind him, and slide the apron around his waist. It's pink, and frilly, and hilarious. I tie it around his waist, copping a quick feel while I'm at it.

"Kiss the Cook," he recites, reading words that are embroidered across the front with a smile on his lips.

"Don't mind if I do." I push up onto my tiptoes and press a kiss against his lips. "Try not to burn this one, okay?"

With another kiss, Caleb says, "I won't."

I walk back over to the seating area, and sit down opposite Ben and Oliver. I take a sip of the martini Oliver mixed for me earlier, then sink back into the cushions to relax. It's been a while since I've spent any time cooking, and prepping the sides for tonight's meal made my feet ache. It's nice to be off of them for a while.

"Felicity couldn't come?" I ask Ben. Obviously, she couldn't, but I'm asking mainly because I want to see Oliver's reaction. He doesn't disappoint, perking up at the sound of her name, then immediately trying to hide it.

"She had a client with an emergency," he says. "She's sorry she couldn't come, but she'll be here next time."

"Assuming there is a next time," Oliver replies.

"I heard that!" Caleb shouts.

"I meant you to!"

"Hey Caleb," Ben says, as he slides up to the edge of his seat. "Did you get the invite for that architectural society thing?"

"Which thing?"

"The benefit to raise money to preserve that old building?" Ben replies.

"How specific," I tease.

"I don't know," Caleb says, flipping a steak. "I'll check with my secretary. Why?"

"It's because Marisa Blake is on the board," Oliver replies.

Ben purses his lips together, looking a little…shamed? Bashful? I can't quite place it. Oliver is grinning like a fool, and Caleb looks incredibly interested in this development. "Even after the thing with her parents?"

"Yep," Oliver replies. "I think they're keeping her on to avoid a drawing attention to her. That thing with her parents isn't her fault, you know? And if they drop her, it'll be a thing."

"Who's Marisa Blake? And what did her parents do?" I ask.

"Marisa Blake is Ben's one that got away. And her parents embezzled a shitload of money," Oliver explains.

"Marisa Blake, huh?" Caleb says. "Are you asking if I'll be your wingman, or…"

"He needs someone to be a buffer so she doesn't punch him in the face the second she sees him," Oliver says, laughing.

"What happened?" I ask.

Ben rubs at the back of his neck. "She was my girlfriend during an…immature phase in my life."

Caleb laughs. "That's one way of putting it."

"Like we didn't all have one?" Ben asks defensively. Caleb and Oliver have the decency to look a little ashamed. "I...I didn't treat her very well. I was too stupid to know what I had then."

"He cheated on her." The expression on Caleb's face tells me that he did not approve, and even though I know he would never, ever do that to me, the fact that he's so openly disdainful of it brings me comfort. "A lot."

"Ben. Ew." That's the only thing I can manage.

"I know, I know. I've regretted it ever since. She was smart, and capable, and beautiful," he says, with a wistful look in his eyes.

"And she was really good to you," Oliver reminds him.

"That too."

"You want to see her at this benefit?" I ask. "Make things right?"

Ben blows out a long, steady breath. "I'd like to try. We were always really...passionate. Fiery."

Oliver raises a brow, then brings his beer up to his lips. "That's one way of putting it."

"We get together, and it's like...all sense goes out the window. And then reality sets in. It's...difficult. But that was my fault, for not being ready for her when she was ready for me."

"You should at least apologize to her," I tell him.

Ben scoffs at me.

"What?" I ask.

"I need to do more than that," he says.

"Obviously. But it starts with an apology. I mean, if you're sorry, apologize. The rest comes after that."

Oliver leans over the arm of the sofa. "Are you paying attention to this, Caleb?"

Caleb turns toward us, and taps his forehead with the handle of the tongs he's holding. "Got it."

I lean forward, hoping Ben will take my advice. "Apologize to her, and see what happens. You're never going to get what you want unless you're willing to go after it," I tell him, giving a pointed look to Oliver while I'm at it. Out of the two of them, I think Oliver's the one who needs to take that advice to heart the most.

"I'm still going to need a buffer."

"Or ten," Oliver teases.

"Caleb and I will go," I tell Ben. When Caleb shoots me a questioning look over his shoulders, I smile at him, imploring him to agree.

"Okay," Caleb says. "We'll go."

"Why do you have that dopey smile on your face?" I ask, bumping my hip against Caleb's as he hands me a clean, wet plate to dry.

"I don't have dopey smiles, okay?" he replies, with

yet another dopey smile. He motions to his face, with suds dripping off of his fingers. "This face is incapable of looking dopey."

"If you say so." Even though he's being petulant, I stretch up onto my tiptoes and give him a kiss.

"What was that for?"

"For not setting anything on fire," I reply, teasing.

"I should not set anything on fire more often."

"I think that's a good plan."

Caleb flicks some sudsy water at me. I let out an accidental squeal, then wipe my face on his shirt.

"Oh," he says, laughing. "Now you're in for it."

Caleb tickles me with wet hands, his fingers trailing their way up my sides. I'm laughing, and squirming my way out of his grip, begging for mercy in no time. He lifts me up and sets me down on the countertop in front of him, settling himself between my legs before he plants his hands on either side of my hips, and leans down for a kiss.

"We hosted our first dinner," he says, smiling against my lips.

"We did."

"We should do it more often."

I brush my nose against his cheek, then kiss him again. I think kissing him is probably one of my favorite things. "We should. You could hone your cooking skills."

"I could." Caleb's fingertips trail along the collar of my

shirt, tickling and brushing, just a tease. "Got any other skills you think need honing?" With his hands on my hips, he slides me forward until I'm perched on the edge of the counter. He rocks his hips, creating a little bit of friction in the best place.

I close my eyes, and let out a soft moan. "Nope. I think those skills are honed. Honed, honed, honed."

"Good to know."

"Hey," I say, sliding my fingers through his thick hair, and gently pulling back so I can look him in the eye.

"Yeah?" His eyes are half-lidded and lust-addled, and when he licks his lips, I'm almost done for.

"Do you have a one that got away?"

Caleb sobers almost immediately, and gives his head a little shake. "What?"

It's something that's been on my mind since our pre-dinner conversation, when Ben mentioned that this Marisa person was his. "You heard me," I say, sliding my hand down the side of his neck. "Did you have your own Marisa Blake? Is there a one that got away from you?"

"Mmm. Yes," he replies. "Almost."

My stomach falls, but curiosity gets the better of me. "What happened?"

"She left me a note on the counter, telling me she was going to turn herself in to a hitman," he replies, letting the pad of his thumb skim across my chin.

"Oh," I reply, feeling a warm, fuzzy relief wash over me.

"She sounds pretty amazing."

"Yeah." He leans in and kisses me softly. "I think I'll keep her."

"She'll probably let you."

"She'll definitely let me when she sees the surprise I have in store for her," he replies with a wicked grin.

"Oooh." I reach for the top button of his jeans, and let out a disappointed noise when he steps away.

Caleb walks over to the refrigerator, and pulls out a perfectly folded brown paper bag.

"What's that?" I ask.

"I made you lunch," he replies proudly. "For your first day of work."

My heart does this little swoop right in my chest, and manages to skip a beat in the process. I find myself tearing up, which is a little ridiculous. It's just lunch. A sandwich, probably, and some cut up vegetables. Maybe that hummus I like. It's the thought of Caleb planning it out, standing at the counter making something for me that's just…it's so sweet I almost can't stand it.

"Thank you," I reply. There's a waver in my voice, and Caleb catches it.

"It's just a sandwich," he says, like he's trying to temper my expectations. Like those expectations ever would've included something gourmet.

I hop off the counter, take the bag, and put it back in the

refrigerator. Then I loop my arms around his neck, and give him a kiss. "Thank you for the just a sandwich," I tell him.

"I wanted to make sure you were alert all day, so you'd be ready to come home and celebrate."

"Oh?" I nip at his chin, because I know how much he likes that. "How are we going to celebrate?"

"I've got a few ideas, don't you worry. C'mon." He takes my hand, flips off the kitchen light, and leads me back to the bedroom.

"Are we getting started early?"

Caleb laughs. "No," he says, catching me by surprise as he pins me against the wall, pressing his body against mine. He leans in like he's going to kiss me, but he's *just* out of reach. A slow grin stretches across his lips as he pulls away. Tease. "Let's go to bed. You need your rest, I want you to have a good day tomorrow."

"Okay," I reply, following his lead.

With Caleb, I know *all* my tomorrows are gonna be good ones.

About the Author

Cassie Cross is a Maryland native and a romantic at heart, who lives outside of Baltimore with her two dogs and a closet full of shoes. Cassie's fondness for swoon-worthy men and strong women are the inspiration for most of her stories, and when she's not busy writing a book, you'll probably find her eating takeout and indulging in her love of 80's sitcoms.

Cassie loves hearing from her readers, so please follow her on Twitter (@ CrossWrites) or leave a review for this book on the site you purchased it from. Thank you!

Printed in Great Britain
by Amazon